GHOST MAN

Donnelle McGee

SIBLING RIVALRY PRESS
LITTLE ROCK, ARKANSAS

WWW.SIBLINGRIVALRYPRESS.COM

Ghost Man
Copyright © 2015 by Donnelle McGee

Author photo by Carmen Pegan
Cover design by Seth Pennington

Sibling Rivalry Press, LLC
PO Box 26147
Little Rock, AR 72221

info@siblingrivalrypress.com

www.siblingrivalrypress.com

ISBN: 978-1-937420-98-7

Library of Congress Control Number: 2015952006

This title is housed permanently in the Rare Books and Special Collections Vault of the Library of Congress.

First Sibling Rivalry Press Edition, November 2015

FOR

MY KIDS WHO ALWAYS KEEP ME GROUNDED:
I LOVE YOU BOTH WITH ALL MY SOUL.

&

JONATHAN AND TOM
WHO GAVE ME PEACE.

Part One
SINKING

My body's dissolution, fain to feed
The worms. And so I groaned, and spent my strength
Until, all passion spent, I lay full length
And quivered like a flayed and bleeding thing.

– Countee Cullen

-VERONICA-

The man on the phone said he wanted a beautiful girl. Had to be fit. And could she come to his hotel room as soon as possible?

I can be there in about an hour.
What do you charge?
Three-hundred-dollar donation.
Okay.

Veronica stood transfixed, feeling as if her feet were stuck in a pool of ice water. Numb and heavy. She looked at the door—Room 217.

Another lost man. And here I go again. What the fuck? I'm getting paid. Just let this dude cum. Be his fantasy, and then get the fuck out of here.

Hi.

He ran his tongue nervously over his thin lips. The man, pushing close to three hundred pounds, was unshaven, and Veronica could see tiny bumps, a sea of swollen, red shaving bumps on his face and neck. He was stripped down to his underwear. Veronica looked past the man into the room. A queen-size bed. A small table with two chairs. A beige, square phone sat on a nightstand to the left of the bed. On the television, she watched two naked women touch one another's breasts.

I see you already started, eh?

Veronica stepped inside the room. The man shut the door.

Hi, I'm Veronica.

The man could not take his eyes off her. His tongue intensified its pace around his lips, only pausing when he grinded his teeth together.

I need the donation before we start.

He presented her with a stack of folded twenty-dollar bills. Veronica unfolded each twenty with the precision of a surgeon so that each bill lay smooth in her palms. When the count was right, she put the wad of cash in the front zipper pocket of her backpack.

Go ahead and lay down on your back.

He quickly took off his underwear and settled himself on the bed. Veronica stood at the edge of the bed, looking at the naked body before her. The only article left on the man's body was a gold wedding band.

Veronica removed a pink scrunchie wrapped around her ponytail, letting her brown hair fall softly to her bony shoulders. She took off her top, slid out of her black sandals, and slowly undid the silver buttons that ran down the front of her white jeans.

You are really pretty.

Without saying a word, she touched her hair away

from her face. Only in panties, Veronica climbed on top of the man and began to move her pelvis around in a frenzied pace. She knew after a short while he would cum and she would be on to her next trick.

She moved her eyes away from the headboard of the bed and over at the digital clock on the nightstand.

Red glare. 8:10 PM.

Come on you desperate motherfucker, go ahead and cum already, hurry the fuck up.

Her night just beginning.

- J U L I U S -

Julius parked his ordinary compact between two faded, white lines. Caught a glimpse of himself in the rear view mirror. Placed his index fingers just below each eye socket and gently stretched the skin downwards. Not even 40. Drained. Releasing his fingers, Julius allowed the skin to regain its natural form.

Wake the fuck up.

He lowered his head, letting it thump against the steering wheel. The thumping turned into a forceful, rhythmic pounding, each successive *bam* harder; the imprint of the steering wheel visible across his forehead.

I'm so fucking weak.

Julius hit the steering wheel hard enough for the horn of his car to sound.

Hey. Hey! Julius.

Julius heard the voice of the man he called an hour ago and slowly lifted his head off the steering wheel. Turned his focus to his left and peered out of the dirty, bird-shit splattered window.

J, you alright?

Julius shook his head up and down. *I'm a mess* sat in his belly. Before opening the car door Julius took a long look at Lyle. He'd woken him at 4:00 AM. He did not know where to turn.

Before you close the door, don't forget your keys, man.

Lyle could see the bronze key ring dangling from the ignition. Scattered on the passenger seat and the floor of the car were ripped out Yellow Pages and crumbled newspaper sections with pictures of skimpy dressed women on them.

Oh yeah. Right you are.

What's going on, J?

Julius reached into his car, grabbed his keys, and shut the door. He put one of the keys into the car's door lock and turned it until the little gray, plastic rectangle piece could drop no further into its slot.

This baby here is an oldie. None of that beep, beep, beep alarm shit. Grace's car has all the fuddy-duddy gadgets. All those bells and whistles give me a damn headache, you know?

Lyle managed a grin.

Sorry for waking you in the middle of the night. Thanks for coming, though. I hope I didn't wake up Stacy.

You woke her.

Damn. Sorry again.

Lyle looked Julius in the eyes. Distant. Dull. The two men leaned against Julius' cream Ford Fiesta. Lyle ran his pinkie through the brown whiskers of his goatee as he spoke.

You want to go inside and get some breakfast?

Julius was relieved that Lyle broke the silence. Dry mounds of despair and shame rolled in Julius' throat, simmering and looking for a fire that was off in the horizon to come and blaze away the ache pummeling throughout his body.

I'm really fucked up. Been like this for a while. But yeah, let's go inside.

It was just after 5:00 AM. The Pancake House had an audience. Julius and Lyle stood in front of the restaurant's wait-to-be-seated sign taking in the smells of eggs, pancakes, and whiffs of hot coffee.

How many? Two?

Damn, Julius thought. *Can't she see there are just two of us here? Do you see three or four? Why would she even ask such a stupid ass question? Patience. Be patient man.*

Yes, two. Thanks.

The hostess, a middle-aged woman with brunette hair held snug on top of her head with bobby pins, escorted Julius and Lyle to a booth and placed two menus on the table.

Can I start you two off with some juice or coffee?

Just some water for now, please.

Lyle looked at Julius.

Water's good.

Julius carefully took his silverware off the white napkin and placed the fork, spoon, and knife on the table.

He slowly unfolded the napkin and rested it on his lap. Then he leaned in as close as he could to Lyle from across the table. Julius closed his eyes and took a deep breath.

I'm fucking up.

Before he could go on, Julius saw out of the corner of his eye the brunette woman approaching.

Here you go.

She sat two glasses filled with crushed ice and water in front of each man.

Your waitress will be right with you.

When the woman left, Julius closed his eyes again and continued.

For most of my life, no ... really all of my life, at least all of it that I can remember, I've been scared. But damn, the last eleven or so, man I've wasted so much money. So much time. Hurt Grace. I've been unfaithful too, Lyle. Lied to the people that are close to me. I have a tough time coping with everyday shit, not to mention trying to deal with my past. But last night, shit, this morning, I bellied up. Hit bottom. I thought about killing myself. Killing myself ran amuck in me. Man, it was all up in me, in and out of my head. Scared the shit out of me.

Hello, are you ready to order?

Julius hadn't even glanced at the menu. Lyle, temporarily frozen from Julius' words, quickly opened a menu, more for effect, not really looking at the listings of entrées.

I'll take ... um, um, well ... how about a stack of

buttermilk pancakes.

Short stack or large stack?

Large.

Anything to drink?

No, the water is fine.

And you sir?

Julius looked at the woman.

How did she end up working at a Pancake House? Working at five in the morning? Was this a full-time job for her or a career? She couldn't be more than thirty-six, maybe thirty-seven. What was her story?

He looked into her brown eyes. She was attractive. She seemed so happy and energetic for so early in the day. The smile she presented the two friends seemed genuine.

I'll just have the pancake sandwich.

How would you like your eggs?

Scrambled, please.

Bacon or sausage?

Bacon.

And a drink?

Orange juice would be nice.

Anything else?

Nope, that'll do it.

As she turned and headed to the kitchen, Julius fought the urge to take a long stare at her slender figure.

J ... you said you thought about killing yourself? Come on now, man.

The thought entered my mind. It's like I'm out of

control. I escape reality all the time. Block out all the mundane shit in my life, you know, all the things that make me feel as if I'm already dead. You know like getting up in the morning, going to work, pumping gas, trying to make my marriage work, and there's so much more. But you know how I get through?

How?

I've been feeding this deadness in my life with the excitement of women, intrigue, fantasy, and sex. Some people would call me a fuckin' sex addict. Lyle, I haven't been home all night.

You talk to Grace?

Nope.

- G R A C E -

Grace was done crying. Done trying to help her husband. Finished watching him destroy their marriage. Julius sucked the life out of her. As she lay alone on their queen-size bed in the middle of the night, she thought about the man she loved.

This man can't give me what I want. I give and give. Nothing comes back.

The alarm clock on Grace's nightstand glared deep green.

1:38 AM.

No Julius.

2:47 AM.

No Julius.

3:30 AM.

No Julius.

No phone call.

Nothing.

Just darkness.

He's not coming home.

Grace imagined Julius driving the streets, cruising for a prostitute. She saw him at a grungy Motel 6 waiting for a call girl or some escort to arrive. There he was at some adult bookstore, feeding quarters into a video machine and masturbating in secret. Wherever he was, he made a choice to be there and not at home in bed with her.

5 AM.

Grace got out of bed. The bottom of the black silk nightgown she wore fell softly down to her bare knees. She walked on the solid maple floor to her closet and reached for the bulky turquoise robe that hung on a plastic hook on the door. Grace made her way to her son's room, where she tiptoed in and gently placed a kiss on his warm cheek.

I love you, Joey.

She ended up in the kitchen. Back and forth she paced. Past the stainless steel refrigerator. Past the toaster oven, the electric can opener, the stove, and oven. Grace circled the kitchen. Each time she walked by the refrigerator she took a quick peek at a picture, held fixed onto the fridge with a Goofy magnet, of her, Joey, and Julius, smiling. They looked like a happy family. *Perception*, she thought, *always good at masking pain.* Grace stopped her nervous walking and sat down at the kitchen table. She put her left hand over her eyes ... *how in the hell did I get here?*

- JULIUS -

Julius' plate of food went untouched. He continued to share with Lyle all of the shame he carried inside of him. Lyle listened with amazement. At times he listened in a state of uncomfortable silence.

Lyle thought he knew his friend well. He met Julius in college, and their friendship was sincere and trustworthy. Still, he was blown away with the stories and the honesty Julius was sharing.

Lyle, there are days when I have to masturbate just to get my ass to work. Just to get my depressed ass in the shower to try and face the day. It's how I cope. Cope with depression.

I never knew.

I know you didn't. Julius ... right ... happy-go-lucky Julius. Right? Smiling, people-pleasing Julius. That's part of me. But really, you know that's not me at all. Shit, I'm trying to escape reality as often as possible. I have a hard time being the Julius people perceive or expect. There are times, man, when I want to run. Leave this planet for a while. Pretend I don't exist.

I never knew.

I got issues Lyle.

Are you going to eat Julius?

Nope. You want it?

Julius handed his plate of food to Lyle.

Damn! You can eat, man.

Lyle removed the bacon strips from Julius' plate, soaked the pancakes and scrambled eggs with strawberry syrup, and attacked the plate of food, more out of the anxiety he felt in his stomach from hearing Julius' truth than for his own hunger. As he chewed, he felt Julius' eyes on him.

Go ahead. So what happened last night ... this morning?

Julius raised his right hand to where he thought his heart might be. He could feel the inside of his body moving, shifting under his flesh. Death on him. The hollowness of his life suffocating him, moving in like an awaited storm, slowly but steadily, and there was nothing he thought he could do to halt it. In his mind he understood the concept of the walking dead. All those people, going about their everyday routines, gutting it out, making every effort to pretend that the next day would be better or at least different. Julius was keen at identifying people like this. They were all around him.

I spent the last six hours in a motel room. Haven't been home. My marriage is over. I'm tired man. Tired of my life.

Lyle pushed the half-eaten plate of food aside and stared at Julius.

I think I'm too weak to commit suicide. Don't worry about me, Lyle. Shit, I called three call girls to visit my room throughout the night. Each time one left I called another. Three hundred bucks a pop too. Shit's expensive, you know? The women came and made their money. Each time I came I felt alive. Saw myself for that brief time connected to my soul; I could feel my pulse.

Julius paused and bowed his head, letting his chin rest on his chest.

I don't know where to go from here. This fuckn' road I'm on has no outlets that I can see.

He took a sip of water, scratched his forehead, licked his lips, and looked at Lyle. The silence at the table was broken by the waitress checking to see if there was anything else she could get for the two men.

Nope, I think we're all done here.

She removed the plates in front of Lyle and gave Julius a concerned look.

Everything alright?

Julius met her brown eyes with his.

Not really, but thanks for asking.

Julius let his eyes slide from her eyes to her name tag.

Monica.

Then to her breast. Then back to her eyes.

Monica put the check on the center of the table and laid two peppermint candies on top.

You two gentlemen have a beautiful day.

Julius cracked his knuckles on the back of his head,

releasing the tension in his body.

That woman is alive.

What?

Her. Monica. You can see it. Her eyes. She has a zest about herself. She's alive, how I admire that. I need that feeling in me.

Look, man, life is ... things that we sift through give us a chance to learn. I sound like a damn therapist. What I mean is that maybe all this shit is giving you a chance to look at yourself, get some help.

Lyle felt his chest quicken. He felt the wetness on top of his pink palms and the dampness taking over his underarms. Julius' truth swam in his head. *He is addicted to women to help him cum so he can momentarily escape reality.*

What about seeing a therapist? Have you considered that?

Yeah, I've thought about it. I'm open to it. Shit, I've been down that path before and, well, you see me now.

Stacy may know someone. I'll check and see.

Julius had mentally already left the conversation and started thinking about how he could get his next hit, his next release. He had to decrease the increasing anxiety and doom crawling up on him. Releasing the hot tension in his body was all he could think about.

Where you heading from here?

Julius studied Lyle's warm eyes.

I need to go home and see Grace.

- G R A C E -

The sun started to rise over the weeping birch that Grace and Julius planted together twelve years ago; it was their first year of marriage. Grace squinted from the sun's rays as she peered outside the sliding glass door into the backyard. She heard the sprinklers come on and saw spirals of water spray up and out before landing quietly on the soft, green grass. She and Julius had turned the soil and laid the sod.

Their marriage was rocketing to its end. And while Grace accepted this, her heart still rose for the man she fell in love with during her last years of college. Yet Grace was a big believer in the certainty of situations.

He's an addict, and he will always be one.

Stability and consistency were part of Grace's psyche. Uncertainty and desperation were part of Julius'. Grace made up her mind. The moment Julius returned home, she would tell him. Tell him that their marriage dies each time he goes off to fantasy land to escape from whatever is torturing him. Tell him that no longer will she sit and wait for him to get sober. And she was done hearing him tell her he was sorry. Tired of seeing him walk around the house looking tentative and lost. The days of watching the man she loves destroy himself were over.

Grace would look him in the eyes and speak above the pain hammering on her, just missing her head, but still taking her down, invisible dents on flesh. She would let him know that her life is crumbling, and it is time that she stood on her own foundation, free of him. She would hear no more promises.

No more *this is the last time*. No more *I have no control over this*. No more bullshit.

When he enters this house I will end this union.

End the wondering if her husband would make it home from work without visiting a massage parlor or stopping in for a lap dance. No more being lied to only to find out later the burning, stinging truth.

Grace laid her head on the table and felt the right side of her face come into contact with the cool, smooth wood.

Rest now.

Strength.

Courage.

Please take this ache from my heart.

-VERONICA-

Veronica rushed down the steps leading away from the motel room. Her next trick was set for 9:00 PM This time she was heading to a house out in the suburbs. The man who called said he wanted a young girl. Slender. Athletic. Veronica opened the driver side door of her car and climbed into the quietness of its interior. She loved the new car smell. The scent awakened her, snapping her back into the present and taking her mind farther away from the things that went on in room 217.

Veronica turned the key and heard the hum of the engine. After turning on the interior dome light, she read the directions to her next destination that she printed out on her home computer a few hours before.

Dome light off.

Veronica pushed the number three button on the CD player. Selected track eleven. Sade. And her skin went soft. Her mind, now a butterfly floating to nowhere in particular, gliding outside of its soul.

Veronica! Veronica! Where are you going?
Away from here.
Honey, where are you going to go? Come back here. You

come back here mija.

Mommy, no. No. I'm tired of it all. And you don't believe me. You don't even believe me. I'm sick of it.

Let's talk about it.

No mas words left mommy. No mas. I'm not going to sit up in that house and watch you drink yourself to death. I'm done. And tell that man, tell that animal, to leave me alone.

Animal? Como?

Look at you. You're drunk now.

Vero, please come back here. Please.

Veronica turned from her mother and walked across the front yard leading away from the door of the duplex. She turned back to look at the woman who gave her life. There her mother stood in the doorway, looking out at her sixteen-year-old daughter. She thought her mother looked both worn and beautiful.

Mommy, I have to go.

Veronica turned off the ignition. Sade's voice disappeared.

Get yourself together, girl. And then she walked up to the door of the cookie cutter home, took a deep breath, and rang the doorbell.

- JULIUS -

Lyle turned right onto Wick Street. Julius turned left. Julius could have made a right too and taken the shorter route to his home.

What the hell?

Release.

Release.

When Julius decided to go home, he knew there would be no more lies. All those half-truths he told Grace over the years would have to be cut up and reshaped into what was real, like truth, them bold daggers drawing the life out of his marriage. He had not gone home last night, and Julius had no intention of heading home now.

Put off going home as long as possible.

Put off the pain of seeing Joey. Avoid, for as long as possible, feeling Grace's disappointment.

Escape this life.

Escape.

Release.

Calmness.

He drove along the quiet street. The sky getting bluer before his eyes.

Left on Marshall.

Drive.

Left on Farleigh.

Drive.

Right on Broadway.

Drive.

Right hand side.

Park.

The yellow sign with red, block letters read 24HR. ADULT BOOKSTORE.

This was a business Julius frequented when it was too early or too late to visit a massage parlor or call an escort service.

Get inside.

Release.

Escape.

Julius reached in the glove box, grabbed a few Kleenex, and stuffed them into his left pant pocket.

Out of car.

Lock it.

Walk.

Release.

Put off the pain for a while.

Don't think about it.

Run my ass away from the gnawing up in me.

Escape my fuckn' insane ass.

Leave this sadness.

Julius pulled the heavy glass door leading into the

bookstore and walked past hundreds of DVDs and VHS tapes.

College Girls Gone Mad

Freaky Suzy

Big Chicks SUCK Dicks

HOLES EVERYWHERE

Amateurs Show All

Hanging above the metal shelves that held the movies, he saw blown-up life-size dolls. Plastic, naked women and men floated in the air. As Julius made his way to the cashier, he swore that the dolls' eyes watched his every move. He was a little freaked out by the dolls, yet they aroused him. He decided he would have to try a doll, see what it felt like to penetrate into one of the plastic vaginas, in the future.

Can I get some change, please?

The man sitting behind the counter looked at him. The man wore a white baseball cap with a red Bud Light logo sewn onto its front. The T-shirt that rested over his chiseled upper body donned an iron-on picture of Superman. "I am Super In Bed" wrapped around the picture.

Julius noticed that he and the man were the only ones in the store.

The cashier remembered seeing Julius in the store a few times.

Anything else I can help you with?

Nope.

Here you go, my man. You let me know if I can help you with anything. Okay? Anything you need you let me know, my man.

Thanks for the change.

Julius turned his back on the man and moved away quickly.

What the fuck is wrong with this guy. Creepy ass dude. My man …

Julius walked to the back of the store, where there were a number of private viewing booths. He looked back toward Superman, now wearing a wide grin that flashed specks of silver and gold.

If I can assist you, just holler, my man. Okay?

I should go.

Doesn't feel right in here.

Fuck it.

Release.

Escape.

Unload.

Kill this beat in my chest.

Inside booth.

Money in.

Take this dollar … come on … take this dollar, machine.

Pick images.

Sound.

Unzip.

Grab.

Hold.

Escape.

No pain.

Pleasure.

Watch.

Beauty.

Grab tighter.

Thrust.

Thrust it.

Thrust it hard and fast.

Fast.

Faster.

Release.

Release.

Again.

Stay in this world. Don't leave it.

Can one of you ladies hold me?

Wrap me in your breasts.

Let me lose touch with the scary world outside.

Grab.

Thrust.

Release.

Unload.

Release.

Again.

Julius sat back in the booth, removed the Kleenex from his pocket, and wiped away his ejaculation as it ran down his dick.

*What the fuck … fuckn' sperm all on my pants and shit …
on the walls … damn floor all sticky and shit. What the fuck.
Shit … shit … shit … Shit. This is my life. Jacking off in
public. I'm fucking ridiculous.*

Julius sat slouched, drained, the excitement of his rush
gone. He was left to sit in his reality. The booth smelled
of fresh semen. He let his shoes move about the floor
beneath him. Dirty. Sticky. The image on the television
in front of him was off now. He saw his reflection on the
screen. He was thankful there was not enough light to
make out the full detail of his face.

Get up, J.

Go home.

Get your pathetic ass up.

Julius sat. Blank stare. Semen on his checkered boxers.
Semen on his pants. Semen scattered around the booth.

This is my life.

Go home.

Be a man.

Get your ass up.

No.

I'll do it again. Fuck it.

Put money in.

Images.

Release.

Escape.

Ease the pain.

Grab.

Tighter.

Thrust.

Faster.

Harder.

Slam my motherfuckn' finger deep up my ass.

Escape.

Release.

Again.

After more than 30 minutes in the booth, Julius figured it was time to depart. He stood up and tried his best to look normal. He had not slept at all the previous night. His eyes showed it. The white around his eyeballs turning pink. In his left eye two minute red dots floated. His wrinkled, blue khakis were stained with semen. The collar on his shirt sagged on one side, unable to keep its upright position. Under his khakis his boxers were damp with semen. The bottom of his shoes stuck ever so slightly to the floor of the booth. He opened the yellow curtain that hung across the narrow entrance into the booth and saw Superman sitting erect on a metal stool not more than five feet away from him.

You have a good time in that booth? I was a little worried about you. You have a good time in there, my man?

What?

Julius carefully stepped around the man, keeping one eye on him and the other on the exit door.

You leaving, my man?

Yeah.

Hold on. Come here.

What the fuck are you doing? Man let go of my fuckn' arm.

I will. But listen here, my man.

Get your fuckn' hands off me.

The grip around Julius' forearm grew tighter. Julius tried to pull away, but now the man held both of his arms. He looked Julius square in the eyes and took a few seconds before he spoke.

Listen. Listen to me real good now.

Man, let go of me.

You been in there for a while. I've been sitting on that stool right there for the last 23 minutes. Your ass is sad. Your ass was in a preview booth so you could preview some of the porn we carry up in here. But oh no, you sit up in there and stroke your dick. What in the fuck is wrong with you, my man? Now, I know when I go in there there's probably going to be cum on the floor, all over the chair and shit. Man, this ain't no motherfuckn' come in and cum shop. I should go make your ass clean that nasty ass shit up right now.

Julius, head lowered, said nothing. He took the verbal assault from the man. He took it like he took life.

Don't confront.

Survive.

The next time you bring your nasty ass in here, I

suggest your keep your dick in your pants. Now, get the fuck out of my store.

Julius felt his arms being released and then go limp. Without saying a word, he shut his eyes. He held them shut as he took a deep breath. Then he opened them and headed for the door leading out. He knew now that he was not ready to head home. He had to find a way to deal with the humiliation. All Julius could mutter as he stepped outside the glass door was kept silent under his tongue.

Crazy ass. Damn, fuck me. Fuck me.

Just find the car.

Get Inside.

Safe.

Julius reached inside the glove box to grab a plastic bottle of antibacterial hand sanitizer. He squirted the clear gel on the palm of his left hand and vigorously rubbed both hands together.

Wash this shit away.

He squirted some more of the hand sanitizer in his left palm, rubbed both hands together again, and began using his hands to wipe his face and neck. To his right, in one of the car's cup holders, sat a plastic water bottle. Julius undid the white cap and splashed water on his pants to see if he could clean the dried spots of semen.

Crazy ass dude.

Go home.

No. No way. Not yet.

Go home. No, that's over.

Fuck me.

How did I get here?

Grace.

Joey.

Help.

Help.

Grace.

Julius started the Fiesta and headed east on Broadway.

- G R A C E -

Hey mom. Where's dad?

Good morning Joey.

Grace stood up from the table and looked at her son. She took him all in. He had Julius' sparkling brown eyes.

Your dad should be home pretty soon.

Where did he go?

You know ... he didn't say. You hungry?

Yes.

Usually on a typical Saturday morning in the Holiday house, Julius would make breakfast. He'd make omelets, pancakes or waffles, bacon, and then he would cut up some fresh fruit to put on the side. Grace always thought he overdid it.

That's too much food Julius.

It's Saturday. It's tradition. Come on Grace, enjoy it. Let's eat.

Too much food, Julius.

Joey, go ahead and get dressed, and I'll make breakfast.

Waffles?

Sure.

Omelets?

Are you that hungry?

Yes.

Sure.

Thanks, mom.

Joey sprinted down the long hallway heading toward his room. Upon reaching his bedroom door, he yelled back to his mom.

Mom, make enough food for dad too.

Grace opened the maple pantry door, grabbed the Bisquick, and sat it on the kitchen island. She found a glass mixing bowl in one of the cabinets. Before she opened the refrigerator to gather up some eggs and milk, she paused to look at another of the many photographs that decorated the doors of the refrigerator. Joey and Julius. Julius holding Joey's arm up in victory. Joey, smiling. Julius, smiling proudly. Joey had just won his third grade class spelling bee.

Where are you, Julius?

Grace thought about calling his cell phone but decided against it.

Where in the world are you, Julius? Fighting them demons?

Grace watched the eggs lose their softness and harden. The aromas of sizzling eggs and crispy, butter-topped waffles filled the house. Grace took down three plates from a cabinet and placed them on the table.

Joey, come on honey, breakfast is just about ready.

Coming.

Joey appeared in the kitchen wearing a big grin.

It smells good in here.

Grace couldn't help but smile. Her eight year old made her happy.

Come on Joey, let's eat.

Joey sat down at the table and took a warm waffle from the plate his mom used to stack the waffles on. Grace served them both a hearty portion of a cheese omelet. She placed a pitcher of orange juice on the table and sat down directly across from her son.

We need syrup. I'll get it.

Joey retrieved the Mrs. Butterworth's from the pantry and sat back down.

Oh, wait.

Where are you going now?

I just need to get the foil like dad does.

Joey ripped off a piece of foil. He made his way back to the table and used the foil to cover the plate stacked with waffles.

Now they won't be cold when dad gets home.

-VERONICA-

Veronica pushed the doorbell again.

Come on now, it's too cold out here.

Again.

Finally the door opened.

Hello.

Come in. No one saw you walk up to the door, right?

What?

No one saw you?

I don't know.

Veronica sized up the trick.

Married.

Kids.

Wife gone for the night with the kids.

Probably early forties. Good job, maybe a teacher.

No. Maybe some tech dude.

Pudgy and nervous but not his first time.

So how are you tonight?

Come in.

Veronica followed her trick through the house until they arrived at a spacious room that most likely served as the family's office and guest room.

Are we going to do it in here?

On the phone you said it cost three-hundred dollars, right?

That's the donation.

He grabbed three one-hundred-dollar bills out of the top drawer of a metal desk pushed up against one of the walls in the room. Veronica could sense that the man was extremely nervous as his hand shook on the exchange of cash between the two.

You can go ahead and get undressed.

Located across the room, opposite the desk, sat a futon. Once undressed, the man made his way toward it. And there he sat.

Naked.

Exposed.

Ready.

Veronica seated herself next to him. Still fully dressed, she bit open the corner of a condom wrapper.

This is for you.

Veronica put the condom on for him.

Oh shit!

The man, baffled and thinking his wife had arrived home unexpectedly from her weekend away, jumped up from the futon wondering what "Oh shit!" meant.

What!

Shit!

What?

Is there a hole in that condom?

What?

Wait. Let me see it. Yep, right there. See it.

What?

There's a hole in the condom. You see it? Right there at the tip.

Oh … I see it.

No problem. Let me get another one. I just bought a pack before I headed over to your house.

Veronica grabbed her backpack and started rummaging through it.

I just bought a brand new pack right on the way here.

Oh good.

Shit, I think I left them in the car. I'll be right back. I'm parked right out front.

Veronica walked toward the front door, still digging through her backpack.

I'll be right back. I'm sorry about this. Be right back sweetie.

Excited about his prospects, his chance to have sex with this young woman, he started to fondle himself. But after about five minutes he started to think that it shouldn't take this long for her to find a pack of condoms. Another minute. And then another. And another.

The man walked to the front of the house. He peeked through white blinds. In front of his house, he saw no car. He saw no sexy woman waiting to reenter his home. And then it hit him like a brick being flung upside his head. And there he was, alone and naked, with a defective condom wrapped around his deflating dick.

- J U L I U S -

The Fiesta rolled down Broadway gliding atop black tar. The sun's rays beamed into the windshield causing Julius to squint. Instead of pulling down the shade visor, Julius took the sun's glare. Hot, yellow light shutting his eyes. The strain on his eyes strong, yet he continued to look straight into the fire. He shifted his eyes away from the sun when his cell phone vibrated through his pant pocket and into his left thigh.

Grace.

Julius pulled the phone out from his pocket and lifted the flap.

Lyle.

Instead of answering, Julius let the call drift to voice mail. And then played the message.

Hey J, giving you a call. Gotta number for you. Stacy knows a therapist who specializes in sexual addictions, and I thought you might be interested. I don't know, maybe it could help. Give me a call when you get this.

Although it was good to hear Lyle's voice, all Julius could focus on was getting to his next *hot spot*. Julius pressed 4 on the phone's keypad. Deleted the message.

Let's see it's about nine. The Victorian should be opening in about thirty minutes.

Getting to The Victorian, a business that Julius visited monthly, sometimes weekly, was his only focus.

Right on Broadway. Past the donut shop. The one he and Joey occasionally came to for hot chocolate and jelly-filled donuts. The Fiesta cruised past a flower shop. Julius saw a gray-haired woman putting yellow, pink, white, and red roses into emerald green baskets. The baskets sat on three glass tables that flanked the entrance into the flower shop. Julius remembered picking out single stem roses from those same emerald green baskets for Grace. He recalled going inside and selecting a small card and writing *Just Because.*

Past CEDRICK'S Steak Place. Past a newspaper stand where two men dressed for a jog stood reading yesterday's news.

Right on Drexel.

Getting closer.

Julius could feel his heart beat quicken like a large river rock inside of a small wooden box being shaken vigorously, the rock ready to break free of its borders. Unable to dodge the course he was moving towards, all Julius was left with was the rapid chatter bouncing in his cranium.

Why am I going here?

I don't want to go home.

Not ready to deal.

Victorian. Nice massage.

Escape.

Then head home.

Shoot this shit out of me over and over again.

Left on Alberta.

Julius held the steering wheel with his left hand. His right hand rested on the hand brake. His eyes fixed on the landscape before him. *Get to The Victorian.* The feelings associated with his crumbling marriage were too hard to digest. The idea of living much of the rest of his life inside massage parlors, cheap motels, and adult bookstores was too fierce to take in. The thought that he felt boiling in his belly was of Joey thinking of him as some crazed-out man. It made his whole body twitch.

Shit, there it is.

Scattered along Alberta were old, massive Victorian homes. Many of the grand homes over the last decade had been renovated and turned into businesses. The Victorian was painted a luscious red with soft pink trim decorating the outer edges of the two-story house. Above the enormous solid oak door with an elegant purple stained glass center hung a sign that read:

THE VICTORIAN
"A Unique Massage Experience"

The sign was suspended on two heavy gold chain links that allowed it to float above the entrance. Julius drove to the back of the business and parked his Fiesta. He checked the time on his cell phone.

9:18 AM.

12 minutes. I'll be alright.

Julius sat and stared at the back door that led into the house.

Julius, come here.

Julius looked up at his mother.

Is Jessica bothering you?

Yeah, she keeps poking me in the face and flicking her fingers on top of my head.

Julius, five years old, could sense his mother was different. The words she spoke to him were a little hard to understand, and she smelled like the "gold stuff" in the clear plastic cup she held in her left hand.

After sitting down at the kitchen table, she motioned for her son to step into the kitchen. Julius, from where he stood at the entryway leading away from the house's front door, stepped on the faded yellow linoleum floor and made his way into the kitchen. Once inside he saw two other adults seated at a square black card table.

Jessica ... Jessica.

Jessica, a year older than Julius, looked into her mother's brown eyes.

You bothering your brother?

No. Tell him to stop teasing me, though.

You bothering your brother little girl?

No.

He said you're flicking and poking at him.

Jessica looked at her mother.

Their eyes meeting and locking.

Tell you what, since you want to poke your brother in the face and flick your hands on his head and you Julius ... you so interested in teasing your sister, then the both of you can fight this shit out.

Tears began to take shape in Julius' eyes.

Go on. You both so tough and shit.

I don't want to fight him momma.

You so tough then go ahead Jessica.

Jessica watched her mother's friends seated at the table pass a joint. The sharp scent made her nose twitch. Tears trickled down both sides of her face. Julius loved the smell of a joint. It both relaxed him and saddened him. But when his mother smoked weed, Julius did not like being around her.

Julius and Jessica stood two feet apart from each other. Julius could smell the flavor of the watermelon gum she chewed.

Shoulders squared.

Julius clinched fists.

Jessica opened hands.

Shit, you kids think you so tough. Go on, what you going to do now?

Julius' heart thumped. He looked at his sister and then to his mother seated at the table. He looked at the two adults seated at the table with his mother.

Gerald and Marjorie. He knew them.

One time Gerald and Marjorie babysat him and Jessica. As soon as their mother left for the evening, Marjorie ordered both kids to their room.

Put your pajamas on and keep your little asses in that room.

Marjorie closed the door. Julius and Jessica could hear Gerald and Marjorie laughing. They could hear music blaring from their mother's stereo. From under the door the smell of weed crept into the room they shared. They could hear Marjorie saying *Fuck me, Gerald. Fuck me.*

Now Julius stared hard at Gerald and Marjorie. His eyes distant but focused on them. He didn't like either of them. He didn't like how his mother was acting. So Julius lashed out at the only person in the room who could feel his pain. The two kids rolled around on the linoleum floor swinging wildly at each other. At one point Julius pinned Jessica on her back and thrust his fist into the side of her head.

Let me up you punk. Let me up.

Jessica freed herself and swung a flurry of punches hitting her brother in his left eye, right arm, and upper left shoulder.

Okay. Shit … that's enough now.

Julius wrestled Jessica back down to the floor. Trying to prevent Julius from climbing on top of her, Jessica kicked at his chest and head.

That's enough damnit! Boy, get off your sister. Stop it. Both of you stop it. Now go on. Get out of here. Go. Go put your pajamas on. Go.

Jessica walked out of the kitchen. Julius stood in front of his mother's chair.

His chest rising up, down, up, down. His curly, red hair scattered all over his head.

I said go on now, Julius.

Julius could not move. His quick breathing and whimpering becoming louder.

He looked his mother in the eyes.

Julius go on now. I'm busy.

He held his focus on his mother. Nothing came from her.

I'm busy. Go on, move it out.

Julius walked out of the kitchen to find his sister.

9:32 AM.

Julius walked from the back parking lot of The Victorian toward the front of the business. He realized that eventually he would have to go home.

Deal with Grace.

End a marriage. Maybe save it though. Save a marriage.

Look Joey in the eyes and tell him why dad would not be home when he woke in the morning. Maybe save a marriage and avoid that talk with Joey.

He spotted a tiny blue jay perched on a fragile branch growing out the core of an oak tree.

How can any living thing be so still and peaceful?

He studied the pretty shades of blue covering the bird's small, oval body. Julius stood flat footed and stared. He watched the bird lift itself from the branch and float into the clear blue sky away from The Victorian, away from him.

Hi.

Hello. Um, do you have any openings?

Yes we do, but it will be about ten minutes or so.

Cool.

Did you want a half an hour or hour massage?

Um, let me get one hour please.

Alright. That's going to be sixty dollars for the hour.

Julius handed the woman seated behind the mahogany counter three twenty-dollar bills. He looked at her and almost asked if she was available to give a massage this morning. He knew better. He learned over time that at most massage parlors the ladies rotated between massage time and counter duty. He stared into her soft blue eyes.

Go ahead and have a seat. Simone will be with you shortly.

Thanks.

Hanging on the walls inside The Victorian's waiting area were reprints of paintings showing plump white women dressed in large puffy dresses holding umbrellas to shield the sun. Two high arch back old-style Victorian chairs, covered in a glistening maroon satin fabric, rested on each side of a gas fireplace. Next to each chair were wooden end tables stained to match the mahogany counter. Julius seated himself in the chair directly across from the woman at the counter. He rested his shoes on the plush, cream carpet below and took a deep breath. Hanging on two nails above the woman's head was a magnetic sign. White letters and numbers stuck on a solid black background.

WELCOME TO THE VICTORIAN
30 Minute Massage = $30.00
60 Minute Massage = $60.00
THANK YOU

Julius didn't recall having ever received a massage from Simone before.

Simone … Simone … she must be new. Who is this woman at the counter? She must be new too.

Attempting to divert his eyes from the woman at the counter, Julius closed them and concentrated on the calming music coming from the ceiling speakers.

He contemplated about his lot in life.

College graduate.

Steady job that he liked. Didn't love it but liked it.

Nice home.

Grace.

Beautiful Grace.

Joey, his world.

Julius let the music enter his body. He could feel the sounds of waves crashing at his feet.

Cleanse me. Wash me.

Hi there. You ready?

Julius opened his eyes to see a woman in her early twenties standing in front of him. He met her green eyes with a closed mouth grin.

Ready.

Follow me.

The pair walked away from the waiting area through two French doors which opened into a wide hallway. The young lady escorted her customer into one of the seven small rooms scattered along the hallway.

Do you want to shower first?

I'm good. Maybe after.

I'm Simone.

Hi Simone. Nice to meet you.

You can get undressed and I'll be right back.

Over the last fifteen years, Julius received more than a hundred massages. His body had been touched by women who he found to be repulsive, attractive, heavy, thin, nice body, not-so-nice body, pretty eyes, mangled face, buff, young, and old. Then there was the occasional woman who blew his mind.

He thought of how gorgeous Simone looked. Maybe 5'6", jet-black straight hair parted in the center of her head. Hair that reached her lower back. The skirt she wore highlighted her strong, defined legs. After he pulled off his clothes and lay up on the elevated twin mattress, Simone tapped on the door before reentering the room. After dimming the light, she slipped off her heels and stepped toward Julius.

You ready?

Ready.

Would you like me to use some oil?

No that's alright.

Julius felt Simone's warm hands touch him high on his back. Very gentle. Each hand rubbing a shoulder blade.

You been here before?

Lots of times. You must be new.

I've been here for a couple of weeks.

Simone moved her hands down to the center of Julius' back. Her tiny hands moved apart then came back together creating a V on his back. The hands separated again ... reunited ... separated ... reunited.

You have a nice body.

Thanks.

Julius figured she was just being polite trying to past the time or buttering him up for a tip.

Do you exercise or anything?

A little bit. You?

No, not really. I'm taking a hip-hop class at school though.

Cool. You're in college then?

JC. Taking some classes.

Are you planning to transfer to a university or?

I don't know. Thought about it. Trying to earn my cosmetology certificate at the moment.

You'll get it.

I don't know. We'll see.

Julius felt the hands on his back slide down across his ass and rest on his hamstrings. Simone gently rubbed each hamstring, then each calf before moving to his feet.

What do you do?

Julius thought about the question for a few seconds.

I cheat on my wife. That's what I do. I frequent massage parlors and masturbate.

I visit strip clubs. Masturbate in adult bookstores. Let's see. Rent porn and masturbate.

Go on the Internet and masturbate. Chat on the phone and fantasize with strangers and masturbate.

Pay for the company of women and masturbate. That's what I do.

It's alright if you don't want to say.

No ... I sell cars.

The hands glided from the feet back up to the neck.

That feels nice.

Good.

Simone slid her hands southward on Julius' body until she reached his ass where she started to maneuver her manicured finger nails along his skin. She let her nails creep off his ass onto his inner thighs. Julius savored the rush of the blood building in the center of his body. Lost in fantasy. Lost in the rhythm of Simone's hands.

You want to turn over onto your back?

Julius rolled over, closed his eyes and waited for her hands to come into contact with his body. Eyes open now, he saw Simone, felt her hair graze lightly against his hairy chest. Hands moved passed his nipples to his stomach around his rib cage down to his thighs and back to his pink nipples where Simone stimulated each to a peak. Then back down to his pubic hair, hands stopping before coming into contact with his penis.

Do you want some oil?

No, No, I'm okay.

By asking that question, Julius knew now that it was okay to masturbate in Simone's presence. The Victorian was a classy massage parlor. The women working there, at least the ones Julius had encountered over the years, were usually alright with a paying customer releasing a load. And on some occasions, if a customer gave a big enough tip, he was treated to view bare breasts or take a long look at a G-String.

Simone's fingers circled his inner thighs nipping his snug scrotum.

Nice.

Magical hands.

Grip.

Slowly.

Hold.

Simone's hands accelerated along his body before settling at his nipples where she pinched each with force.

Nice.

Thrust.

Eyes closed. Eyes open.

See her beautiful face.

Smell her scent.

Pineapple.

Coconut.

Not too fast.

Make this moment last as long as possible.

Done.

Let me get you a hot towel.

Simone left Julius naked in the room with semen on his belly, now beginning to slide down both sides of his pelvic bone.

Over.

The moment over.

And damn, numb again.

Big bad ass reality staring my ass in the face.

Simone returned with a hot cotton towel and wiped away the semen.

- G R A C E -

Did you get enough?

I did.

That's good Joey. Go ahead and clear your plate if you're done please.

Joey walked over to the kitchen sink, turned on the faucet and watched the maple syrup slide from his plate and into the drain.

What time is Van's party mom?

I believe his party is at 1. But double check. The invitation is on the fridge.

I see it.

I'm going to hop in the shower. If you could clear the table and wipe down the counters please. I'll take care of the dishes.

Mom you're right, it's at 1.

Okay, that's what I thought.

Grace walked out of the kitchen.

Face the day Grace.

The shower felt good. Warm water raced down her caramel-colored body. She heard the constant, soothing sound of the water as it sprayed free of the nickel-plated head. She let her shoulders droop.

Relax. At least for a moment.

Grace knew her husband's plight was not about her. Not about her body, looks, or how she treated him. It never had been.

Julius and Grace met at the library during their third year in college. A chance meeting they would say years later.

Mind if we join you?

The young woman looked up from the poetry journal in her hands and saw two men looking down at her.

Hey Robbie. How are you doing?

Good Good. Can we sit?

Okay.

Grace this is J. J that's Grace.

What you working on?

Reading some poetry.

Cool Cool. You like it?

You know … I do. Taking this creative writing class this quarter and yeah, I like the whole poetry vibe.

Cool Cool. J and me are about to knock out some of this math homework.

Grace studied Robbie's friend. Beautiful eyes. Alive. She remembered seeing him in the campus center a couple of times. Nice, lean body.

J transferred in from JC. He's roommates with Ronald.

Ronald? Ronald Duke?

Yep Yep.

Man. I haven't spoken with big R in a while. I thought he—

Dropped out?

No, I was thinking kicked out.

Naw. He was close to being kicked out of here. His coach and he worked it out. He's still here.

That's good.

Playing ball?

Yep Yep.

You play J?

I play. Not on the team but I play some.

Grace once again glanced at his eyes.

Well, I'll let you two tackle that math.

After their meeting in the library, Grace saw J three days later, even though she was hoping to run into him on campus much sooner. She saw Robbie one evening during an intramural volleyball game and was disappointed that J was not with him.

How's your friend?

Who, J?

Yes.

Good Good.

Where does he hang out on campus?

I don't keep tabs on him or nothing like that. He's a little little quiet. You know you know he kinda keeps to himself at times. He's good people people you know?

I'll take your word.

You lookin' for him, huh? Okay Okay. I got you I got you. Naw I'm playing with you. He eats in the campus center usually. Besides that, he's either in class, he has a work study job over in the financial aid office, or you can find him in the library sometimes sometimes.

Can I join you?

J, right?

Right.

Sit down.

Grace watched J pull the shoulder straps of his backpack off his broad back and rest it on the laminated wood table.

Where's Robbie?

He was supposed to meet me here but I don't know. No show. You seen him?

Nope Nope.

Maybe he'll show later.

Cool Cool.

Why you clowning on Robbie?

Yep Yep.

Look at you laughing at my friend Robbie. That's cold.

Naw Naw.

Grace couldn't hold back her laughter. It wasn't the first time she had made fun of Robbie's speech tendencies.

The jokes are out tonight. What are you reading tonight?

I'm writing tonight.

Well I'm reading tonight.

Cool Cool.

Grace you are a fool.

He remembered my name. Grace smiled.

Thank you J Thank you J. But really J., Robbie and I are good friends. I tease him all the time and he's alright with it.

Well okay, I'll let you write.

And I'll let you read.

Thank you, Grace. I appreciate your kindness.

My pleasure J. But J?

Yeah.

Grace held her stare in his eyes.

J. Is your name J like J   A   Y   or is it Jason or J for short or just J?

My name is Julius.

Like it. Like it.

You look nice mom.

Thank you, Joey. That was really a sweet thing to say honey. My little gentleman.

When do you think dad is coming home? I wonder if he'll be home before the party.

Let's call him and see.

The shower had relaxed Grace, gave her a renewed outlook. She was ready to deal with what was in front of her. Twelve years of marriage was on the brink. Her green eyes, deep and soothing like the jade she wore around her neck, glistened with new energy as she grabbed the cordless phone from its holder. *It is time to honestly face my marriage. No more of them wasted days slippin' by my feet. No more hoping that things will get better. No more holding on to how it could be. No more trying to change this man. Shit, I can't save him.*

Is it ringing?

Yes.

Answer your phone Julius.

He will mom.

Hello, you've reached Julius. Please leave a message and I will call you back as soon as possible. Have a beautiful day.

Hi Julius. Joey and I are calling to see when you plan on coming in. Remember, Joey is going to Van's party at 1 today. Okay then, I guess we'll see you soon.

Grace pushed the off button on the phone.

Joey looked at his mom.

Voicemail?

Just voicemail Joey.

Grace never liked seeing her son worried or cheerless, particularly when it was due to Julius. She could sense the uncertainty in Joey.

Well ... say you and me knock out these dishes and get on with our day.

I already wiped down the counters and cleared the table.

I see. Alright, give me about twenty minutes to finish up. And we still need to get Van a birthday gift. Any ideas?

He likes to play wiffle ball. He really likes sports.

What else?

Um ... we trade our football and baseball cards. He likes those a lot.

Okay then. We'll find something nice for Mr. Van.

- J U L I U S -

Julius lifted the flap of his cell phone to check the time and saw he had a missed call.

Grace.

It was Saturday. Approaching 11:00 AM. He had not been home since he left for work early Friday morning.

Julius knew before he laid down next to Grace on Thursday night that he would not be heading to work the next day. On Thursday night, like many of the nights in his home, his heart raced. He felt tension, pressure, and a pain that needed to be released from his body.

Are you doing okay Julius?

Yeah I'm fine.

You sure?

I'm fine.

Julius, we can talk about what you're feeling or we can just talk about how you are doing. You seem preoccupied. What's going on with you?

I'm fine. Really.

Really?

Really.

I'm going to bed.

Julius watched Grace leave the room and move toward the hallway leading to their bedroom.

Quiet. Julius sat on the couch in the family room, left only with himself. He didn't understand why he couldn't open up to Grace on a consistent basis. He spent the next ten minutes in his head. Every couple of minutes he jabbed his fists into his forehead, the internal dialogue accelerating his urge to escape from his body.

Did I marry the right woman?

I can't give myself fully to this woman.

I'm so fucking weak.

When I am going to stop living this lie?

I can't fully commit to this marriage.

I can't stop escaping.

Julius heard the soft hum coming from the refrigerator. Solitude. Too still for Julius. Too much time to think. There was too much time for the deadening heaviness of his life to move from the deep caves within his body. Too much time for the images of his past to swing before his eyes. Stillness made his palms sweat and his chest pound. There were times when the motionlessness caused his torso to jerk unexpectedly, all the pent-up energy making every attempt to find an outlet to bathe in. If a surgeon cut open his chest, Julius knew then he would be able to see the layers of shame, grime, and slippery specimens surrounding his heart. He knew that each time his heart beat, the worm-like creatures moved in closer. He could feel them slithering inside of him. He could smell the funk on their wet backs. He could hear their hissing. Their voices in his head.

Deal with us or we will eat your ass alive.

For Julius, there were days when being cut-off from the real world, cut-off from stillness and sadness, was what he most needed. Friday would be one of those days. A sexual holiday.

And now Grace had called. Left a message. Time to go home. The bender coming to a close. Julius was not ready to hear Grace's voice, even her recorded voice. He decided to make one last stop and then head home to face Grace.

Part Two
SCARS

Girl you are rich
Even with nothing
You know tenderness
Comes from pain
It's amazing how you love
And love is kind
And love can give
And get no gain
It's down a rugged road
You've come …

It's Only Love That Gets You Through

– Sade

-VERONICA-

Veronica you're home?

I got nowhere to go Mommy. Nowhere I want to go anyway.

He's gone.

For how long this time?

He's gone. Vero, I didn't realize ...

That's because you're drinking too much. You're not yourself enough. Mommy what's wrong with our life?

Our life is what it is.

Mommy, you don't work a normal job. You don't want to work.

We have a house. We have food. Where I come from, I'd say we are doing fine mija.

And we have an eviction notice duct-taped to our front door too. Do you know what that means? Wake up.

I'm aware of it and I will handle that.

I'm tired of moving.

Before opening her mouth to speak again, Veronica's mother dug her eyes deep into her firstborn. She saw a scared little girl, barely sixteen, and her eyes already losing their gleam.

Her daughter's heart hardening before her. Veronica was pissed off more often than not. Pissed off at life. At her. What could she say to her daughter now? Just thirty-one years old.

It was true, she had no steady job. She used her body to make money. She used the money she earned to buy alcohol. She collected her welfare funds and gave the food stamps to Veronica to buy groceries. She ached for the little boy who left her arms nine days after his birth. If she believed it, she would tell Veronica that everything was going to be all right. Life will get better. Easier. She and Veronica would move to a nicer part of the city and get off welfare.

Mommy would enter one of those twelve-step programs and live the rest of her life in bliss. Be sober for the next forty years. She would be a proud grandmother. Yet Katrina knew life was bumpy and harsh. This was the world she lived in. All she could muster up to say to her daughter pained her. But she said it anyway.

You better learn to deal with life mija.

What?

You heard me. Cope. You gotta deal with what you got. I'm tired too. But I deal.

Right, okay. You deal with your drinking.

Like I said, I deal.

You can deal so much better mommy.

I'm just outta gas mija. I'm tired.

You're young.

Maybe you'll do better with your life mija.

The next morning Veronica was awakened by a loud pounding coming from the front door.

Okay. Okay. Okay! Here I come. Stop the pounding. I'm

here.

I'm with the Mowry County Marshall's Office. Is there an adult here?

Veronica studied the lean man with the gun on his right hip.

I'm barely awake here. What do you need?

I need to speak with your mom or ... dad. Is there an adult here?

Veronica let her eyes move from the Marshall to her right where her mother was passed out on the couch. There she was, in full sprawl, wearing just panties and a bra, with the television on and an opened bottle of Boones on the faded rug below her.

There she is. I've got to get out of here.

Well, that's why I am here. I'm going to need to wake her.

- J U L I U S -

Julius parked across the street from the Ridge Stone apartment complex. He stared into the blue sky outside the windshield of the Fiesta. The sun was beginning to drift higher into the rich blueness. The glare not as intense as earlier.

Okay J. Let's go.

After a deep breath, he tapped his heart with his right hand, made a peace sign with the same hand, and brought the two fingers to his dry, pink lips.

Much love. Need much love.

Ridge Stone, built in the 1960s, was rundown. More than forty units, mostly one and two bedroom spaces, were located within its structure. In the center of the complex was a pool with no water in it. The units framed the pool. Residents could look from their front door, whether on the first or second floor, and eyeball the entire cement community. Julius climbed the peeling, white cement painted stairs at the northeast corner of the complex that led to the second floor. At the top of the stairs, he turned right and walked slowly to door #37. He pushed the black square lodged on the center of the door.

No answer.

Again.

Wait.

No answer.

Julius checked the number above the doorbell again. #37.

This time he knocked on the door.

Who is it?

It's Julius.

Who?

It's Julius. It's me. Julius.

As the door started to open, Julius' heart raced. He could smell his childhood. The woman at the door smiled. Missing from her mouth was her big front left tooth, knocked completely out by a former boyfriend. Her brown eyes no longer vibrant, now dim and sinking back into their sockets. The woman looked at Julius.

Come in little J. This is a surprise, this really is a surprise.

It was approaching noon. A long, satin, black nightgown covered the woman's skinny frame.

Come in Julius. Come on. Get in here.

Looking over her shoulder he saw darkness.

Did I wake you?

Julius walked into the apartment. It looked as it always did. Dark and dusty. A couch with a faded green and white checkered blanket swung over the top, a glass coffee table where someone's fingerprints had created polka dots on its surface. He could see that the sink in the kitchen was full of dishes, probably there for a couple of days. The carpet beneath his shoes and the linoleum in the kitchen were filthy.

Julius shut his eyes. He fought every urge in his body to begin to clean the tiny apartment.

I was up.

It's dark in here. You plan on letting some lights shine up in here?

Jessica flipped on a light switch. Julius hoped she would open the curtains. It was still too dark for him.

What you been up to Julius? How is Grace? Joey? You doing well? You talked to Eileen lately? How you doing Julius?

Julius did not know where to start.

I just came by to see how you are.

I will always be okay. You know me. I'm a survivor, boy.

I know you are Jess.

Julius, you looked in the mirror lately?

Why do you say that?

You look like you been up all night. You look all tired and strung out.

How is Eileen?

She's alive. She asked about you.

She has my phone number.

Jessica, still a little tipsy from the night before, walked up to her brother. Julius was turned away from her, looking at a framed picture of the two of them that was taken in a motel parking lot.

Julius 9, Jessica 10, their eyes fixed on the person holding the camera. Both kids, wet from the rain, showing little expression.

Jessica put her hands on his shoulders.

Why you so jumpy?

Just don't sneak up on me.

Sneak up on you? What the hell …

Why do you keep this depressing picture in your apartment?

That there, that picture right there is part of our story bru. Look, you came here for something right? Let it out. Come on.

No. Just came to see how you are doing.

Okay Julius, right. Julius, you walking heavy up in here today.

Do you like your life?

It's the life I got Julius.

You happy, I mean is your soul cool?

You getting pretty deep J. But I know what you mean and I tell you what. My rent is paid this month. I'm not turning tricks on the street. I have a little money in my pocket. So yes, I mean I'm not in fucking celebration mode, but shit I'm hanging in there.

Julius looked at his sister. He tried not to judge her. In the end, he couldn't help himself. Here she was. The day was half over and she was not dressed. She had alcohol on her breath. Her house was filthy. How could she be doing okay? How could she be anywhere near happy?

What about your soul? How you feeling? You happy bru?

I'm here. I get through and get over what I have to.

Shit, you doing more than getting through. You got a beautiful little family. Making good college money. I'd be celebrating my ass off on a daily basis if I was you. But I know you too. And you hold on to a lot of stuff that isn't your fault. You got to let that shit out Julius. Every time you come by my place you look like the whole damn world is on your shoulders. Do you want to talk? You want to get things out in the open? What, Julius? What has you looking so drained when your life is a good one? You have a good life. Look at you. You been here for more than twenty minutes and you have yet to sit down. Sit down; you make me nervous hovering like you are.

I have to go.

Yeah, okay. You come back when you want to talk. Wait, wait now Julius, wait now, you going to take my picture? I mean it's cool. If you need that image to begin to deal with the shit that is fucking your life up, then take it.

I don't want this picture. You need anything?

No, Julius. No. I just hope the next time I see you that you look a lot lighter.

I have to go Jess. Here's your picture. Maybe it's time I go see Eileen?

Julius made his way back to his car. Not ready to get in or pull away from Jessica's apartment, he took a seat on the curb. He thought about Jessica and how she had the nerve to take an inventory of his life.

Maybe she should look at her own fucked-up life before analyzing mine.

He sat on the curb facing his sister's apartment complex. He watched a father and son walk by him on the sidewalk. The son decked out in little league gear. White pants dirtied on the knees. White shirt with Dodgers written across the chest. Blue hat with a white cursive D in the center.

Julius thought of Joey. He watched two hummingbirds dance together around three blooming pink and lavender crate myrtles planted in front of Ridge Stone. Life was all around him and he felt like a man walking to a buffet already full. Already bloated. Already dead. The stuffing away of a miserable life.

What did Jessica know about letting the shit out? And what did she know about my existence?

Not your fault. Not your fault. Fuck. It was my fault.

Julius stood up from the curb. He knew that Jessica was part of the *shit* that he was holding in and how chaotic their sibling relationship had been as kids. But she wanted him to shake things out into the open.

As he moved to enter his car, Julius let a small smile overcome him.

Jessica is right. It's time to let loose these demons.

The penetrating voice of his sister rang in his ears as he made the drive home.

-VERONICA-

Veronica's next performance was not until 11 PM. That left her a little more than an hour and a half to drive home and say goodnight to Sabrina. She felt a tinge of guilt about getting over on the man in the suburbs. But he was an easy target. And she knew he would not call the police. He looked too jumpy and timid to try any retaliation against her for taking his three hundred dollars. That was part of the business as far as Veronica was concerned. Every now and then—and she had only done this to two other men over her five-year run as a call girl—it was nice to make some easy money without having to sleep with a trick, stick a dildo into various holes on her body or the tricks', and who knows what else.

Veronica lived in a new housing development in Ratham, away from the large city of Bluechester. Ratham was becoming a housing haven for professionals who worked in Bluechester but couldn't afford the outrageous housing prices that made Bluechester one of the most expensive landscapes in the United States. Ratham, a small city with a population of a little more than 57,000, along with Caspet, Elms, and Bluff City, all less than 100 miles from Bluechester, offered affordable housing, great schools, and a grinding commute into Bluechester.

On most days when Veronica pushed the garage door opener, she couldn't help but smile. Her home was more than 2,400 square feet, had tile floors, granite countertops in the kitchen, hardwood floors in some rooms, and berber carpet in others.

Who would have thought this up? I'm a fuckn' homeowner.

On the days when she didn't smile, Veronica thought about what she did for a living. She thought about how she was able to afford to live in a home like the one she did. She seldom criticized her choice of profession. Sure, she would like to be doing something that she could talk freely about to her neighbors. Instead, her job was secret. This bothered her.

Hey Lucy, everything fine?

Hey girl, everything is fine. She was trying to wait up for you but faded out about oh … I guess about twenty, thirty minutes ago or so. You going back out?

I got one at 11.

Well I'll be here all night and Inez should be in here at about 1. That's what she told me the last time I talked with her anyway.

Alridey. Let me go check on my girl.

Veronica slipped her feet out of her sandals and sat them on the floor by the couch in the family room. She liked how the texture of the hardwood felt on her bare feet as she walked down the hallway to her daughter's room. Opening the door the first thing she saw was her daughter's night light, a little girl illuminated in a tutu and ballerina slippers, and then she saw Sabrina. Eyes closed, head resting partly on her left arm and partly on a puffy pillow. Her right arm dangled freely off the side of her twin bed.

Veronica took a seat on the carpet next to the bed. She put both hands under her chin and watched Sabrina sleep. Hearing Sabrina's breathing relaxed her. She was so close she could feel the air leaving Sabrina's nose and then make its way to her own face before disappearing into the quietness of the room.

If Veronica could she would sit there all night, like she had done on the night when she was nearly raped in a Cloud 8 motel room by a man who wanted more than she was willing to provide.

She knew she would have to leave soon for her next performance. And there was a chance there could be a couple of more performances after that. Maybe she would be home by 3 AM. Like so many nights before, Veronica would come home in the wee morning hours, catch a few hours of sleep and when Sabrina awoke she used every ounce of energy in her body to be fully present with her daughter. This was her life. The days were Sabrina's and the majority of the nights were for the men.

The sound coming from her left pocket startled her. *Oh shit.*

Veronica fumbled with the cell phone hitting one of the buttons to silence the noise. Even though it was Sade singing smoothly to alert her she had an incoming call, the noise still broke the tranquility of the room. Veronica turned the phone off hoping Sabrina's sleep was not interrupted. She watched her six year old move ever so slightly in the bed. Veronica let out a smile. She could eat up Sabrina. She was her butterfly. In whispers she began to tell Sabrina of the plan she had.

Maybe another year or so. I'll be doing something that will make you proud. Be home at night with you more often and you won't have to be with so many different people when mommy is not here.

Too many people coming and going in this house. Thank you for being the strong angel you are. And not judging me. Maybe I'll go back to school. I'm smart. I promise you I will always be here with you. Wherever I go mija, you are in my heart at every turn. Thank you for being in my life. I love you and I can't wait to see you in the morning. Mommy will be here when you wake up. I promise that. Night. I could sit here all night with you Sabrina. But I can't tonight.

Lucy gently touched the top of Veronica's head.

Hey girl, Veronica ... nightshift time. Veronica ...

Dang. Okay. Just rested the eyes for a minute. What time is it?

Close to 11. Is the hotel close?

It's over in Caspet. I can be there in twenty.

Well you got twenty.

I'll make it. Shit, make the sucka wait a little bit for me, you know?

- GRACE -

Let me get Van's gift.

Grace lifted the hatch of the Honda Accord, reached into the trunk and grabbed an orange gift bag with green tissue paper bursting on all sides.

Come on. I'll walk you inside.

Van's mother answered the door wearing a frazzled smile.

Hello Joey. Hi Grace. Come on in you two.

How are you Mai?

I'll tell you, for throwing a birthday party I'm doing well.

The house was decorated in festive red and yellow. Giant helium-filled balloons were scattered throughout the house resting up against vaulted white ceilings.

The kids are out at the pool.

Hey Joey!

Joey liked Van's dad. He coached the little league team that he and Van played on last spring. Joey liked how he was always happy. And he liked the times when Van and his dad would come pick him up and take him to the batting cages to hit hundreds of dirty rubber baseballs into big black nets.

Hi Coach.

Here, Grace let me take that for you.

Mai and her husband led Joey and Grace to the backyard. Mai paused for a second to set the gift bag on a coffee table in the family's entertainment room which led into the backyard.

Allow me.

Coach pulled open the sliding glass door letting Joey, Grace, and Mai onto a redwood deck that overlooked a rectangle swimming pool. Pine and maple trees were in the corners of the yard. Flowers colored vibrant pinks, whites, purples, and yellows were on display throughout the yard.

It looks beautiful back here.

Well thank you, but all the credit goes to our gardeners. If I could, as Mai will tell you, I would love to spend a lot more time out here in the yard. Having my hands in the soil is refreshing.

Van climbed out of the pool and ran over to Joey.

Please walk son.

You coming in Joey?

Joey looked up at his mom for approval.

Sensing a little uneasiness in Grace, Mai motioned over to where Annie, Van's sixteen-year-old sister, and a girlfriend of hers were seated in lawn chairs eyeing the kids in the water. Joey could tread water but he wasn't a good swimmer by any means and seeing the two young ladies allowed Grace to relax some. Grace had little patience around water and never found a need to submerge herself in it, even on blistering summer days in Caspet.

You have a good time Joey.

Grace kissed him on the cheek.

I'll be back to pick you up in a couple of hours.

With some time to herself, Grace decided not to go back home but rather to sit at her favorite bookstore, sip on a tall banana shake, and write some poetry. Writing poetry was what Grace did.

Grace Holiday was an emerging poet ever since she won Bostonville's prestigious *Write Away* first poetry book contest two years ago. By winning the contest, coveted by so many American poets, she had her first collection published by Bostonville Press. Grace was also flown to Boston to give a public reading of her work. And Bostonville Press agreed to publish her second collection, a book of poetry and prose, which was due to be in bookstores in a matter of months.

Grace had begun submitting her poems, at the urging of Julius, to magazines during her last year of undergraduate school. It took a year or so and a lot of work with her craft, but her poems started being accepted by editors and began appearing in a variety of poetry journals. After she earned her Masters of Fine Arts degree in creative writing, Grace kept writing and took an adjunct faculty teaching position at Luther College, the college where both she and Julius graduated from. Still employed at Luther, Grace was more than excited to have her first book of poetry published, and she never thought she would one day have a second book of poetry float out and into the world.

Each time she walked into Journey Bookstore, her face warmed at just the thought of knowing she could stroll over to the poetry section and locate a little book that held within it her words. And now Coolstar Press, a reputable publishing house on the east coast, awaited Grace's almost completed third manuscript.

Grace pulled the handle toward her and walked through the large glass door making her way into the bookstore. Journey was a midsize bookstore. One would not call it a mom-and-pop or a good old quaint and comfy place, yet it wasn't an enormous book warehouse with a trendy coffee shop smack in the middle of it either. Journey was the place that Grace retreated to when it was time to write. She headed directly to her favorite spot, a black leather chair placed directly in the middle of the psychology section. If on occasion, her first choice area was occupied, then she would head toward the children's section to find a corner and sit like a pretzel atop the bright orange Astroturf that radiated from the floor.

Grace, already with a banana shake in hand purchased next door at the Ice Cream Stop, let her petite frame sink into the chair. She set the shake off to her right on the carpet and pulled out a blue medium ball point pen and a red Mead composition book from her oversized purse. Grace sat there for a few moments allowing her eyes to wander the shelves before her.

Eyes glancing at titles:

The Feeling Good Handbook.

Overcoming Anxiety.

The New Male Sexuality.

Out of the Shadows ... and on and on her eyes met spines of books.

Grace opened the composition book to a blank page. Still her eyes diverted back to the stacks of self-help books surrounding her. It was not by accident that Grace took anchor in this section of the bookstore to create her poetry.

She thought about Julius then gripped the pen tighter and wrote:

J

good man lost

on

bad road

beat

and

i sit

waiting

like the lioness

ready to move

in for the kill
if not
then
i become
prey

Grace turned the page to find a clean sheet. Her thoughts still with Julius she wrote:

PREY.

-VERONICA-

It was 11:10 PM when she drove her silver Mustang into the Best Western parking lot. She punched in a number on her cell phone and waited.

Hello.

I'm here, which room are you in again?

Oh um ... I'm on the second floor ...

Yeah ... okay, but what number?

Not another dumb ass. It's too late to be dealing with a nervous burro.

Julius, embarrassed, opened the door, peeked out to read the number on front of the door.

42.

What? 4 what? Can you talk a little louder?

It's room 42. Number 42.

I'll be up in a minute.

Do you take credit ca ...

All he heard was a dial tone. Julius had spent more than three hundred dollars since he called into work sick on Friday morning. He wanted to get the most out of his sexual holiday. He had been to two strip clubs and three massage parlors. Semen left his dick five times already today. And he wanted to be sure that he could pay for the sixth time with plastic. He had forgotten to ask the young lady on the phone when he set up the appointment if he could pay with a credit card. And if he could not then he was out of luck because he already had maxed out his daily cash withdrawal limit at his bank.

As the young lady approached his hotel room, Julius tried to ready himself. The words moving fast in his head. Words coming fast. Words and thoughts scattered. Frantic.

She sounded pretty on the phone but you never know let's see should I stay dressed naked no that looks desperate TV on music channel Spanish show I think she is Latin porn to set the tone no no porn channels in this hotel ER Red Sox Yanks hope she takes my credit card I really want to cum I'm a little nervous here come on man you've done this many times relax have not been home all day did not call God I'm a fuck up fucked up Grace Joey going to sleep where the fuck am I do you know where your kid's daddy is shit lights on off what if she's a cop shit no I've used this escort service before but

Veronica that's her name never met her let me stroke it a little give it a little size before she comes where is she at said a minute shit she's not going to show probably best take my ass home I'm married what the fuck is up with this this is some powerful pull got me all strung out the whole day wasted cash on seconds of shooting sperm in the air fuck me hope she is pretty sexy at least she should be here let me check the peep hole she's not coming I'm going to have to call a different service hope she's not one of those ugly ones all aged and weathered in the business past their prime

I sound pathetic be happy with what you get shit for 300 hundred a pop I want some mother fuckin' snapping beauty to help me escape whatever the fuck it is messing with me ...

When Veronica knocked on the door, Julius lowered the volume of the telenovela on the television, turned off the light over the bathroom sink, and pulled his right hand out of his pants. He glanced through the peep hole and could see Veronica standing there. She was pretty and he really hoped she took credit cards.

You made it.

You're not a cop are you?

No no not a cop but do you take credit cards?

Can I get in the room please eh?

Oh yeah come in. Damn. Sorry.

Is this your first time?

No no no I've used your service before but I think it was called a different name or something but no, it's not my first time doing something like this.

Well we haven't done anything yet.

I know.

You sure you're not a cop? You seem a little jumpy. You just nervous or what?

Veronica looked at her client.

Not a cop but something about him, maybe he's just really nervous. Looks married. Kids and all. I can do this, this is what I do ... this is what I do ... I prefer cash. Do you have cash?

If I had cash why in the hell would I ask you if you took a credit card, shit. No I don't.

You can't use an ATM? There's a bank right across the street.

Maxed that out already.

Oh, okay. This isn't your first time I can see that now. Okay. Well, you know what? What's your name?

J.

Just J like ...

Just J.

I'm Veronica.

Julius was taken aback with Veronica's beauty. Her honey-colored skin, her slim physique, and her eyes reminded him of the amber rocks that sit on top of his desk at work, his good luck rocks.

So J, I don't take credit cards, you know eh?

You don't? The add in the Yellow Pages had a visa logo and master card logo, you sure about that?

I'm sure. So what do you want to do? Do you have cash or what?

You don't take credit cards? How about a debit card or an ATM card?

I take cash J.

Julius' body sagged.

Shit no cash the prettiest call girl I have ever seen and I got no cash to pay her what can I do what can I do ATM can't pull any cash out reached the limit wonder if midnight begins a new day

Veronica, can you wait until midnight?

What?

I think I can pull some cash out then. It's a new day and the bank …

I have other appointments. And if you have no cash then I need to go.

She's gone.

Maybe next time J.

Hold on, I think you are really beautiful … and …

Thank you. But I need cash. If you want, you can give me a call tomorrow.

Julius looked at her. He needed her there with him.

Oh you know what J?

What's that?

I'm just messing around with you. I'll take your credit card.

Julius' white teeth roped the front of his face.

Nervous laughter. Relief. *Why is she playing with me like that man she is a nice young lady though wonder what her story is how did she get to where she is in her life I really wonder but she's taking my credit card damn that's good news*

All cool but let me check and make sure my card hasn't expired.

Cute and you should hope it hasn't. Here, let me see it Mr. J.

Veronica moved further into the room and sat down on the double-size bed closest to the door. She opened her backpack and pulled out a white VeriFone credit card machine.

Just need an outlet and a phone jack and we'll be good.

It's 300 right?

$300 donation.

Veronica moved the nightstand that rested between the two double beds in the room back a foot and removed the phone line from the metallic-covered phone jack in the wall. She then inserted the phone line dangling from the back of the machine into the empty phone jack.

Mágico.

Veronica slid Julius' gold visa card into the machine's card reader. Seated up on the bed, right leg crossed over her left with her right leg twitching slightly, she entered numbers using the machine's keypad and watched the mini screen flash green.

You are approved. Let me print you a receipt.

What will this transaction show up as on my credit card statement?

Veronica looked at Julius for a second.

Just curious.

It's going to say Sexy Ass Veronica's Hot Night Fantasy Show.

What?

I'm just messing with you.

Man she is alive soul is alive.

It will say Touch Haven Concepts. Any more concerns?

Nope.

So J, are you ready?

Julius shook his head to signal yes then watched Veronica neatly put the credit card machine into her backpack. She pushed back the nightstand and set her eyes on Julius, who was standing in front of the television.

You don't really watch this ridiculous shit do you? You know that ain't real life.

And this is?

So which bed you want to do this on? I'm just going to use the bathroom for a minute. Go ahead and undress and lay on your back.

Julius turned off the telenovela. He sat down on the end of the bed furthest from the window. Directly across from the bed hanging on the wall was a large framed mirror. He watched himself become naked. He could see his forty years in his stomach, the softness of his belly real.

Not wanting to make a bad impression he quickly tried to harden his dick, all the while listening for Veronica to vacate the bathroom. He caught his face in the mirror.

This is the choice I make no one to blame but me failure as a husband failure as …

Veronica came out of the bathroom holding two white hand towels and wearing nothing but light blue panties imprinted with a large white star over her vagina. Julius looked up at her and was transcended from his world into another aura he tasted in tiny bits over the years. In her eyes he saw lakes of escape. In her small, firm breasts he saw hope. In her feminine legs he saw the roots he wished he had. And in her smile he wished for better days.

He watched Veronica's cream smile and then felt her

brownness fall on him.

Hi J.

Julius went silent. Still. He let his body follow Veronica's voice then the motion of her body.

Veronica straddled the center of him letting the star on her panties glide into and around his penis. Julius touched both of her nipples as she planted her hands on his chest and gyrated atop him. He watched her hair swing in misdirection. And even though he was not inside her, he felt as if he were.

The motion of her body intensified and Julius hung on by grabbing her bronze shoulders. He let his hands touch her long, smooth back. In a moment or two he knew he would cum, but he wanted this moment to last a lot longer. However, Veronica was good at what she did, and Julius could not hold in his release. He let out a voice mixed with both hope and regret. Veronica felt the warm semen wet the inside of her thighs and run around to her bottom. She rolled off of Julius and watched him clutch then stroke his dick making every attempt to let it all out. Finally, he released his grip on himself and looked over at the young stranger lying next to him who was on her side using her right hand and elbow to prop herself up.

That was beautiful.

Veronica smiled.

For some reason she believed him. A lot of the men she had gotten off over the years said similar things or said nothing at all, just looked at her awkwardly hoping she would leave *yesterday* because they were done with her.

Here's a towel she said, tossing one of the white hand towels to him.

Your hour is not up J, you still have some more time if you want it.

Julius turned his body to face Veronica. Using his left hand and elbow, he propped himself up.

So what do you do for a living J?

What do you think?

I don't know. You're hard to figure.

Veronica was engaging and Julius felt comfortable with her. He was a little surprised because many times before when he was with a call girl, once he came the show was over. He or she would pack it up and head off. But this call girl was telling him he had more time if he wanted it.

Considering that she had just helped him bring an awakening in his body that still tingled his legs, he let his guard down and opened himself to her. He had some time. Paid-for time as it was. It was still time with a woman who was asking about him.

I'm a teacher.

Really? You know I can see that in you. I see a few teachers in my line of work. A lot of them all stressed, built up anxiety, nervous as hell and looking to unload. Most of them married, kids, house, all that stuff. But they still venture out to see me or one of the other girls.

Sounds like me. I'm married. I have a great kid. I still—

And it's cool. At least you're not out having an affair on your wife, going to clubs and whatever and picking up women. Call girls save a lot of marriages.

How's that?

Because this relationship is confidential, you know private. We don't call your house looking for you and most times the wife doesn't even know unless you're the one to slip up somehow or just straight out tell her. And you know what? Sometimes men, shit, women too, need an escape with someone else just to have a little something extra, a little release to fight whatever off … I don't know but I would think marriage can get lonely at times. What do you teach?

History.

My daughter is in elementary school.

My son is too.

Veronica and Julius sat in silence for a moment separated by less than a foot on the bed. Veronica let her eyes peer into Julius. Unable to hold her penetrating look, Julius moved his gaze around the small room.

Do you want to move on to something else in your life?

I got my plan to leave this business real soon here. You laughing at me eh?

Yeah, I'm laughing, but not at you. At me because I'm trying to get over using sex, in whatever form you want to call it—over the phone, porn whatever as a way to cope with and get through life. I run from a lot of things. Sex, masturbation lets me put off reality, it softens the numbness I feel in my body. And even married to a woman that I think I love, you know even trying to surrender it all to her is … it can be pretty complex.

I've never been married. Never even seen it done successfully, if it can be, but I can see how men, how you, can step out on your wife. We all got devils to run from and shit to heal from too.

Julius let her words sit in his head for a few seconds.

Devils to run from. Shit to heal from too.

He couldn't think of a time in his life where he wasn't either running from some scary shit or trying to heal from some scary shit.

You know though, I'm getting tired of running. And I don't really know how to heal because I got some things in my past, my life, that need something, some kind of closure or I don't um I really don't think I'll …

Julius went silent. He and Veronica remained on the bed. Julius calm, naked, and his erection now mellow and soft. Veronica rested her left hand on the elastic of her panties. Both bodies sank slightly into the mattress. Their eyes looked into yet past each other's.

Hey Veronica. Julius' voice all but a whisper.

Veronica let her eyes shift back to Julius. She studied his face. His eyebrows, running across his pale face, lightly touching in the middle. He was so pale that he could be

104

an albino. She let her eyes roam his face, his thick lips and long ladylike eyelashes. His ears seemed too big for the size of his head. His auburn reddish hair interesting. She could tell he made an attempt to take care of his body. His body was long and lean, mostly, but she could see little gatherings of extra skin at his hips and stomach.

Yeah.

I was just wondering. Wondering what you think my story is.

Your story eh? Your story …

Hal le lu jah Hal le lu jah …

Hold on a minute.

Veronica left the bed and walked over to the other bed in the room. She unzipped the front zipper pocket on her backpack and pulled out her cell phone.

What time? I know I know but what time is he talking about?

Hey Veronica.

Veronica turned to face Julius who mouthed three words to her.

1:30? You know what, I'm not done here yet and this is going to be my last one for the night. Just tell him we can get together tomorrow night. Okay? Okay yeah yeah grats.

Veronica put the phone back in her backpack and walked over to Julius.

J, I can stay but you have to pay me. You know that right?

I know that. Thanks for staying. Damn ... and you like Sade?

Oh you caught that eh? Sade heals me man. That woman's voice unravels the shit in my mind, all that garbage of my past you know? But you asked me about your story right?

Julius nodded and watched Veronica lay down next to him on the bed again. He saw a small scar on the top of her right shoulder. It was healed but he could tell it ran deep once. He noticed the slight gap between her front teeth when she spoke and her slight overbite. He took full notice of her narrow feet and he loved how each toe lined up from the big toe to the little toe in descending precision. He took her face in and was in awe of how she wore little, if any, makeup.

So let me see now. Your story. Shit, I could make up something but I don't know J.

Just try. I think you know my story. I think you know all about me and my kind.

I've been with you for less than an hour. I have some impressions about you but I don't really know you.

Give me some of your impressions then.

You really need to know this?

Veronica closed her eyes. Put her left hand on Julius' heart. Held it there for a few seconds before sitting up on the bed and moving to its edge where she sat with her back to Julius. Julius followed the head of a pink dove diving from her lower back into the beginning of her ass and caught a glimpse of its wings disappearing into her panties. He imagined each wing covering equal halves of her firm ass.

Then she spoke quickly. The words zooming from her mouth:

You're scared / married and scared / bet your wife is nice and sweet but something is lost there / I don't know what something / you're sad stressed with yourself bored with yourself scared of yourself or of some shit that haunts you maybe your family maybe you're facing death so you try to find excitement with girls like me before you die / I don't know but you asked for my impressions / you're needy / you lock in your strength like you're afraid to let go to get out of the way of yourself / you live in rooms like these / fantasy / it's a lot easier to be here than to be with your wife / you don't want to feel inside yourself because you might scare the shit out of you so your story J is a story of secrets / pain / you don't want to be here but you gotta be here with girls like me like you need the touch / to cum / but you know paying me to be with you is just fantasy / it fades within the hour and that scares you / my impression of you is that you are a nice man who loves his wife but a man who doesn't know how to be with a woman like that / I don't think you can be in love with her until your get over your own stuff maybe you have some things blocking you from loving / I'm just talking about impressions here J / I could be off just talking here / a lot of what I say could apply to a whole bunch of us but you asked …

Julius kept his eyes on her slender back.

So I'm telling you some things maybe you already know / I've been with a lot of men in rooms like these / most times just some horny ass guy wanting to get off and then some of them maybe the wife or girlfriend won't get wild enough with him / blow him let him ram rough and tough into her / some men want the two girl show some want to crawl on their knees be pissed and shit on or fucked with a strap-on dick / have their ass licked / you name it they ask for it / then men like you J / you just want some company and men like you are the strangest because you're the ones who really are the unhappy / the desperate /the hooked looking for intimacy in a place where you will never find it but you keep coming back for more / we call you easy prey because you gotta have it / need that cum to numb / just my impressions of you / you are that man looking for intimacy in a place where it cannot be found / you can try and you probably have tried the strip clubs the massage houses all that /it's not there J / there's not any intimacy there / this here is a business man / it's a business for profit / no time to fulfill a man's need for mommy's lost love or hold me and understand me / not the place / that place is in a relationship and I'm not one to talk because my personal life is fucked up but

I know in rooms like this men only find at best an escape / a temporary one from the shit that scares the shit out of them and all them unhealed scars still holler at your ass / they ain't went nowhere just because you shot some semen up and out of you and that's all I got to say about impressions / that's it. Shit. That's it.

Veronica rose from the bed and turned to look at Julius.

You have at least fifty minutes left. What do you want to do?

Julius stared at her breasts, not because he wanted to, but because he couldn't look her in the eyes. She knew he was a scared man. All the fantasy of their encounter evaporated from his body. He saw her as a woman now. Julius averted his glare away from Veronica. Here he was again, paying to escape from the shit that made him ache. Acting like a child who pissed in the bed then hid the sheets in the closet only to be found by the angry dad later, Julius put on his boxers then his khakis. He pulled his wallet from the front pocket of his pants. As he opened the wallet he caught the image of a photo. There, held snugly in the see-through vinyl, were Joey and Grace. Joey smiling at something beyond the camera and Grace looking like she had just found utopia. Julius remembered taking this photo of his family. It was Joey's first day of kindergarten. He and Grace were so excited to pick him up. Joey was so proud of himself. *I didn't even cry daddy. I was brave.*

Here's the credit card.

J, we just started the second hour. You sure you don't want to use it?

Nope.

As she ran the credit card through the machine, she noticed how Julius never made eye contact with her. He had lost his spunk. The show was over and she knew it was time to make her exit.

You just need to sign this and then I'll give you your receipt and be outta here.

Veronica figured her impressions of him were right on. She reasoned that she called him out; she burst the fantasy bubble he lived in. Yet she was dumbstruck at Julius' change in personality. Of how he went from open, interesting, and funny to downright *Mr. Depresso*.

Here's your receipt. Hope Saturday morning brings some sun your way.

You too.

Veronica paused at the door to look back into the room.

Hey, I don't judge you man. I really don't. Find the shit that scares the shit out of you. The shit that leads you to rooms like this and you'll stop ending up here all alone. I hope you don't call me again. I mean that in a good way too, eh.

I need help.

We all do.

And then Veronica stepped out of the hotel room closing the door behind her. The click of the door being shut confirmed Julius' worst fear. He was all alone again.

Part Three
GHOST MAN

It's been too hard living, but I'm afraid to die
Cause I don't know what's out there beyond the sky
It's been a long, a long time coming
But I know a change is gonna come, oh yes it will

Change Is Gonna Come

- Sam Cooke

- J U L I U S -

Julius entered his home trying to control the pop pop pop thud inside his chest. He wondered what he would say when he met Grace's eyes. Joey's too. He stood in the entryway of the house and blew out a long breath while bringing his shoulders up to his neck to ease the tension racing through his tired body.

He sensed the house was empty and was relieved that he at least had a little more time before the end of his marriage with Grace was closer to reality. Their years together as a couple flashed in his mind. He reasoned that there were so many more good times than bad. But he knew that when things went bad, when his demons, them worms, rose up inside him, those bad times really crushed the marriage. And things had gone real bad every couple of years.

He walked around the house taking in familiar smells. He entered the hallway and caught a whiff of the sweetness of Grace's perfume. Looking into Joey's room, he loved the stiff zest of the hundred or so books that were situated neatly on two large, white bookshelves. He spent the next twenty or so minutes pacing around his home trying to capture its essence. He looked at family photos. He continued to savor the smells, Grace's clean panties tucked away in her dresser, the hardness of the oak desk in the office, the scent of clean maple floors, and the funk, ever so slightly, escaping the laundry room.

He entered the kitchen. Pulled the Reynolds Wrap off the plate of waffles that sat on the table, took one, and placed the foil back around the plate. The waffle was still warm. He loved Grace's waffles, how she added a touch of vanilla into the batter to create a bit of sweetness with each bite.

The low hum of the garage door opening made its way to Julius. He heard the sound of the engine diminish.

He waited.

He imagined Grace sitting behind the wheel gathering her thoughts. She would have seen his car in the driveway. A long silence seemed to hang between the garage door and the kitchen; a long, empty bridge between Grace and Julius.

Julius stuffed the rest of the waffle into his mouth.

Grace pulled down the vanity mirror in the car. It lit up. She stared at her face.

Her eyes looked back at her. She loved how they sparkled. Even after all the years in an up and down marriage, she never lost the sparkle in her eyes. Grace studied the bags under her eyes. She referred to them as her safety deposit boxes, where she stored the helpless feelings of having a husband who was incapable of leaving a doomed road.

Write Grace. Breathe.

She reached over to the passenger seat and removed a pen and the red composition book from her purse. Words floated in her, moving from her stomach up through her throat and into her head. And she wrote:

LEAVE

Red boots stepping out
and over a halted mind
where I leave the blues.

Grace closed the composition book and set it in her lap. She fanned her fingers over the bags on her face. Then she brought her hands to her ears and touched her earrings. Today she wore her lucky ones. Tiny, 14 karat gold earrings. Not much bigger than a stud. Sitting on each post of the earrings was a dolphin. The earrings were a birthday gift from Julius. He gave them to Grace the night before her twenty-first birthday.

I hope these bring you much luck Ms. Grace Silverman.

Grace held her hand on the dolphins, enjoying how the gold felt as she rubbed it between her thumb and index finger. A surge of energy raced through her breasts. She had a sensation of finding freedom just around the corner. Here was the chance to leave a man who she still loved. This was true. Yet this was more of an opportunity to leave a man who was wearing her down with his promises of a sober tomorrow.

Julius didn't mind that it was taking his wife some time to enter the house.

He had nothing to say anyway. He would listen. Not try to explain. He knew Grace would get fed up with him sooner or later. He loved Grace. He thought she was stunning. It baffled him why she wasn't enough for him, why he was unable to fully give himself to her.

And then they came.

Leave me the fuck alone. Stop the chewing in me, get the fangs off me.

Julius shook his head hoping to shake the worms out of him. Then he heard the first slam, the car door, then the slight vibration of the garage door closing and then the slam of the back door. He closed his eyes. He could hear Grace's footsteps moving toward the kitchen. He smelled her scent. He imagined the beautiful color of her skin. He imagined her face, always nearly make-up free because she didn't need it. He imagined her auburn hair, shaped into a bob, just missing her soft, rounded shoulders. And he imagined what it could have been like if he was able to keep the worms away and instead be the man, the husband he knew Grace wanted.

Julius, you're here.

Grace looked at her husband.

His red hair. His white skin, so white he was thought to be an albino by some, something that Grace knew bothered him. He looked fatigued. The crease in his khakis long gone.

Julius hung his head. Said nothing.

Julius. Julius, please, you can look at me.

Grace was surprised at how calm she was addressing Julius. Her voice was calm. Even with a little compassion. Julius raised his head. Kept his eyes shut.

Look, Julius wherever you have been whatever you have done is your business. In the past I tried to understand why you need to do what you do. We tried to get help for our little family here. You went the twelve-step route for a while. I realize now. I finally realize today, right now in this moment, that if I stay with you, I betray myself.

You want to get a divorce then, right?

Let me finish. Julius can you open your eyes? I'm done. I'm tired of us hiding from one another. I'm done with the life we have created together. I'm stepping away from it. Julius, Julius do you see me here? Do you hear me? I do love you. I don't like what our marriage has become. I don't like how you choose to escape; I believe that is what you call it, escape from life. And I would not like the woman I would become if I just kept sitting up here in this house and pretending that some day you would get healthy. That someday our marriage would get better. What I am saying Julius is that the weight of your addiction or sickness … well what do you call it Julius? Can you answer me that question? Can you?

Some kind of addiction. I don't know …

Well, I don't know either. However, the weight of

living with you is suffocating me. I won't do it anymore. I'm done.

You shouldn't have to Grace.

I know that. You see I did live with it for far too long. And that's my fault. I always thought somehow that you would get better. Maybe if I did this or that.

It's never been about you Grace. It's always about me. About my shame about my demons.

Grace sat down at the kitchen table and motioned to Julius to do the same.

You know what hurts the most is that I'm disappointed in you because I know, I mean I catch glimpses of you, of the man I know I love, only that man appears so infrequently. I only hope for your sake that you're able to find out why you choose to live the way you do. I don't know if it's due to your mom or sister or what. I just don't know because you keep so much sealed up in you. I hope you learn to trust yourself enough. To trust the people in your life that love you. Let me see your hands Julius.

My hands?

Grace put her hands on top of Julius' as if the two were about to partake in a game of hot-hands.

Get the help you need. Do that for yourself Julius.

Hey Grace I'm sorry for ...

Don't be. I was part of this marriage too and the things you were doing gave me the opportunity to leave this marriage a long time ago. I chose to stay. So don't be sorry. You can be sorry for yourself. Because you are about to lose a beautiful woman who loves you but who cannot be with you. Be sorry for that. Don't be sorry for me, though.

Still, I'm still sorry for all the shit I put you through. You know, all the shit with me throwing away our money on women, porn, all those things. I'm sorry for you having to take the HIV test, all the lies …

Julius, you can stop.

Well, I just want to tell you, I, shit I don't know, I just always loved you but I just don't know how to show you and I don't know how to receive your love either.

I know you don't know how Julius. I have known that for a while now. You are a good man Julius. I really hope you discover how to love. I hope you discover how to love yourself.

Grace removed her hands from atop the hands of Julius. The two sat in silence until Julius tapped his fingers on the kitchen table. Grace looked out into the backyard at the rainbow lantanas climbing out of one of the couple's terracotta pots.

I've never been divorced before.

Grace let out a soft giggle. Me neither, Julius.

Julius glanced quickly into Grace's eyes. Bursts of green looking right back at him.

He maneuvered his tongue inside his mouth to free a tiny piece of waffle stuck in his right molar. He knew his marriage was over years ago. Sure, he and Grace had their moments of bliss. Being parents and all the energy that went into providing for Joey gave them the opportunity for a welcome departure from their partner struggles. The two grew good at keeping their marital issues away from Joey.

For the first time in a long time, Julius spoke to Grace with an honesty that alarmed him.

Our marriage was over a while ago and I think me and maybe you too—let me not speak for you. I know how you hate that. But I was too scared to leave, even though I knew I should have. You know, not leave you because I can't stand being married to you. It was more like leave you because I have so much shit to work on in my life and a lot of the shit I think requires me being out of a relationship. I really don't know how to have a good relationship with myself, let alone with you Grace. I thought things would work themselves out. Only I ran to, well you know where I went. All I'm doing is numbing out the shit that needs to be confronted.

Julius ran both of his hands through his hair which he wore short. He thought about Joey. *I like your fade dad. I want to cut my hair like that too.*

I saw Jessica today.

How is she?

Same. What's weird is that she seems happy. And you know how messed up her life is. Then I was thinking that she doesn't see her life as being all a mess. That's how I see it. I asked her if she had heard from Eileen.

Had she?

She said no, but I think she has.

Grace smiled at Julius.

You know for a long time I thought I could change you. I thought I could change your behavior. I didn't understand why you had to visit the places you did, well, the places you still do. I know you pretty well. I know a little about your mom and Jessica. I hope you tap into those relationships. I always felt the answers, if not the reasons why you do what you do, have something to do with your family dynamics. And I am not judging you or your family ...

I know you're not.

Seems like some of the things you told me you endured as a kid in a way explains a lot. I thought on so many occasions. I mean, I believed you over and over again that you could, you would, be able to stop doing what you do and gain some self-control. I realized last night when you didn't come home that it's not about you having self-control. I realized that you must be really hurting, from what I don't know, from a life or a time in your life that haunts you or scares you so much that you retreat from yourself. Retreat from me and Joey.

Joey.

Julius felt his stomach bite at his ribs. It pained him to comprehend how a divorce would impact his son's life.

Separation. Divorce. Seeing Joey on the weekends or once a month. Seeing him on holidays. Julius' mind started to drift.

He looked at Grace with a dumbfounded stare.

Julius! Jessica! Come on now, Aunt Trisha is waiting for you.

Momma, I don't want to go with Aunt Trisha.

Come here Julius.

Seven-year-old Julius sheepishly walked over to his mother. His mother sat on a metal folding chair outside on the patio of the small house she rented.

Julius you too old to be crying now. Look up at me.

Julius wiped away the tears rolling down his face only to feel the wetness of new ones taking their place.

Look at momma. Momma needs to get some things straightened out. I want you to go with your Aunt Trisha and Uncle Bobbie. You'll just be staying with them for a week or two.

But I don't want to go.

You're going Julius.

Julius watched his Uncle Bobbie pack five duffel bags into the back of a green Impala.

Julius, stop crying. I need you to go with your sister. You hear me? Take care of your sister. And you do what your Aunt and Uncle tell you to do too.

Julius' heartbeat hit the walls of his little chest. Each thump caused his shoulders to bounce slightly up toward his neck.

Momma, I want to stay here with you.

No crybabies riding with me. Not in my car.

Bobbie come on now.

I'm just trying to help the boy out Eileen. All that crying ain't going to help. Any more bags?

No that's it.

Okay then. Let's load 'em up.

Jessica came out of the house eating a Hostess crumb cake. Walking right behind her was her aunt.

Eileen I'll have the kids call you when we get in. Let me let you say goodbye to your kids. Trisha walked over to Bobbie who was standing next to the car.

I know she ain't about to eat no messy ass crumb cake in my car.

Shit, Bobbie you're such a neat freak.

Jessica and Julius stood in front of their mother.

You both go on now and be good, you hear me?

Stop that crying Julius.

Jessica grabbed her brother's left hand. And even though she wanted to cry too, she didn't.

Eileen squeezed them both as tight as she could.

I promise you, we will be together soon. Okay? You believe your momma?

Jessica looked up at her mother.

I believe you momma.

You believe me Julius?

Julius held on tightly to his sister's hand and said nothing. Eileen watched her children step down from the patio and walk the short distance to the car.

Jessica, you finish that crumb cake before you get your ass in my car.

Julius looked up at his Uncle Bobbie. He couldn't find the

words to say what he wanted to tell the big man. Instead he looked
back at his mother. And then the big man looked his way.

And Julius you better stop all that damn crying if you plan on
living with me. Why your momma ever kept your little ass I'll
never know. Y'all go ahead and get in the car.

Eileen never rose from the metal chair.

Joey ... hey maybe we could try to work our
differences out, we could ...

Julius we have no differences to work out. You need
to work out how you will stay with the living. You need
to find out how, or maybe why is the better word, why
you so badly have to run off and into the places you find
yourself.

Lyle talked about a therapist who specializes in sexual
escape ... addictions and things. I could start seeing a
therapist again.

Again, Julius?

You know, I don't want to hurt Joey. I can't leave him.

Julius, see the therapist. Do that for yourself. I told
you, I'm done here. Go see the therapist, you know, go
work on yourself.

Grace had been preparing herself for this day for
years. The insides of her body twitched. She thought
there must be a waterfall of tears hiding behind her eyes.
Her toes tingled. The hair under her arms, the hair that
grossed out Julius until he started to find it sexy, stood
erect. Grace presented Julius with a controlled and loving

show on the outside. She knew this was the right decision for her. Her brain told her so. But her heart would hurt for the man who walked into the college library and made her hands sweat.

We could … we could …

No. You and I as husband and wife is not working. Julius we can be friends. I hope we can. You will always be Joey's father. I can't be your wife. The way you live your life does not give me the space to be. The way you live your life, I don't think it gives you the clarity to be you.

I just thought if I had another …

Julius stopped himself. He had told Grace too many times before that if only he could be given one more chance. He told her he would seek help. Get a twelve-step sponsor. He tried everything. None of it helped to stop the worms from creeping into him.

I just thought for Joey's sake that …

No. This is not about Joey. No Julius. No.

I need help Grace. I can't stop doing what I'm doing. I need help. I want to be a good husband, a good father, but all this shit gets in the way, all the pain and shame from I don't know … I'm trying to deal. I need some healing.

Julius rose from his chair and walked over to the sliding glass door looking out into the backyard. He could feel the tears moving down his cheeks. He opened the sliding glass door and savored the scent of the honeysuckle growing along the back fence. Grace watched him and she too felt the tears sliding down the side of her face.

- GRACE -

Grace asked Julius if he minded going to pick up Joey from Van's birthday party.

You'll have a chance to talk to him alone. He'll be happy to see you.

Grace and Julius agreed that they would separate from each other and move toward a formal divorce. They wanted the process to be as smooth as possible for Joey. Julius would move out of the house the following weekend. They would use the week under the same roof to discuss with a lawyer how they envisioned the business side of their divorce. Each would sit down with Joey individually and they would have discussions with him as a couple too. Julius knew that until he could get a grasp on his life the best place for Joey was with Grace.

Until you get a place of your own, you can stay here with Joey on the weekends. I'll make plans to be away.

Now alone in the house she and Julius purchased together, their first home, Grace experienced the realness of her situation. She stepped into the office. She loved this room the most. Book after book lined the mahogany bookshelves. On the floor, not yet put on the shelves, were the newest books just bought last week when Joey,

Julius, and she spent an afternoon at Journey Bookstore. One of the books caught her eye. It sat on top of the stack, which meant that the book would be the next on Grace's reading list. Grace picked up the book. The book's cover struck her. The deep redness of it. The title running vertically on the front of the book read *Ordinary Words*. The author's name, Ruth Stone, ran horizontally across the cover breaking into the space between *Ordinary* and *Words*. What fascinated Grace most about the cover was the shadowy, almost smoky, image of a face, if it was a face. She wasn't sure. With the book still in her hand, Grace sat down on the soft berber carpet. She studied the book's cover trying to make out the image coming out of the redness. After getting up to get a stack of note cards and a pen from the desk, she returned to the floor. With the book in front of her, she lay on her belly and began to write:

ghost man here ghost man come gone ghost man me
Ghost Man come and gone

ME GHOST MAN HAS COME AND GONE

the first time
the curve of your teeter totter worked above me
left me with a sizzle

in my heart
and the redness of your crown
not matching the paleness of your skin
nor the shifting brownness in your eyes
awed me

then your true grit moved from me
into the frenzy
those pink spirals i think only you see
pink spirals rotating
you either laying on the bellies of strangers
or laying on your back
erected for the healing
i could not endure

yes, me ghost man you have come and gone
from inside these thighs
then i tried to cure the ache
in you
me not pretty enough, no
the demons up in you too far
still, if only i could roll
your cry for touch into a
ball that rests inside of me
but i can't do that
as you simmer with the roughness of women
i pass on dark,
dirty city sidewalks

yes, me ghost man you have come and gone
from inside these thighs

then i look at all the grace in you
this is not a surprise
you always brought a purple swiftness into any room
you entered
you carried your imperfections too
worried that the parasites would one day eat you alive
take to your face
and so you ran to LALA land
ran not to me
turned over on your belly to have the hairs of your ass
tickled

yes, me ghost man you have come and gone
from inside these thighs

then you are gone
your smell no longer detectable
its aroma captured
silenced like us
captured like the dreams
that are now just that
dreams moving, like the fiery smoke leaving burning
rubber,
swaying into the beauty of a crisp
blue sky

yes, me ghost man you have come and gone
from inside these thighs

Grace picked up the book and kissed the shadowy image on its cover before putting it back on top of the stack. She looked at the poem she had written and decided to end there for the day. Maybe she would look at it again in a couple of days. Then again she decided, on second thought, what needed to be said was said.

- J U L I U S -

Julius felt at ease with himself as he and Joey rode in the car. The shower he took back at home relaxed him. He yearned for a good sleep, having been up for more than thirty six hours now, but he was happy to see his son. He didn't know what to say to him. The looming talk of a divorce punched him in the gut.

What do I say here? How was the party? Did Van have a good time? Was the cake good? Did you swim?

You want to get something to eat?

I had a lot of pizza at the party dad.

Right, right of course you did.

Is mom at home?

Yeah. I guess we'll head there too.

Julius glanced over at Joey. He seemed content just to be riding along. Hanging with dad.

Julius began to feel a burning sensation in his stomach. He wasn't sure how he would go about telling his son, that come next week he would no longer be living with him. That he would see him a few times a week. The boy's bliss brought tears. Julius wiped at his eyes with his right thumb.

Hey dad.

What's up?

I almost beat Van swimming.

You had a race?

Yes. It was me, Van, and Karen, and I almost beat him. Karen beat us both. She's good.

As Joey talked about the party and what he planned to do when he arrived at home, Julius soaked up every word. Not one to pray a lot, Julius found himself asking *if there is a God or some kind of Spirit somewhere out there, please spare Joey from the heartache, from the demons.*

- VERONICA -

Sunday morning Veronica awoke to the sounds of Sade singing soulfully from her cell phone. She snuggled up against Sabrina and let Sade sing. Again and again, Sade's voice signaled that Veronica had a call coming in on her cell phone.

It's too early for this.

Veronica reached on top of one of the two nightstands beside her queen-size sleigh bed to grab the phone.

Hello.

Vero.

Veronica pulled the covers up on Sabrina.

Vero, Vero are you there?

Veronica's pulse quickened. She recognized the man's voice on the phone. When she left home for good, when she left her mother, he and his wife opened their home to her. And even though she was hardly there, the home served as a resting place, a place to have a good hot meal. But when she turned eighteen, Veronica began stripping at Velvet Jeans, a gentlemen's club. She started to earn enough money to afford to rent her own apartment. While working at the strip club, she discovered the lucrative world of the escort industry.

Veronica always felt a strong sense of love toward her uncle, and a tiny morsel for her quirky aunt, who took her in when she had nowhere to go. It had been more than four years since she moved out of their house and now she rarely saw them. She did make it a tradition to drop off gifts every year during the Christmas season. She mailed birthday and anniversary cards faithfully. So when Veronica heard her uncle's voice, she was surprised and knew something was not quite right. Her uncle, the older brother of her mother, was not the type of person to pick up the phone just to say hello, to see how you were doing.

Uncle Roman?

Vero it's you.

It's me tio.

Vero … it's your mother, you need to come see her y pronto mija.

Is she hurt?

No she's not hurt. You need to come see her anyway. Can you come now Vero?

The last time Veronica saw her mother was the morning she left home. It had been seven years now. The image of her passed-out mother laid out on the floor became vivid. She could still smell the cheap wine hovering over her mother.

In those seven years she had spoken to her on the phone. Most of the calls ended with her mom asking her if she could borrow some money. Each time, Veronica gave her uncle money to give to her. On a few occasions, Veronica attempted to reach out to her mother. The last time was two years ago on Veronica's twenty-first birthday. She called her mother to see if she would like to go to lunch. When she arrived to pick her up, her mother was nowhere to be found.

Hey Uncle Roman, I really don't want to see her. Does she need some money or something, eh?

Her uncle's voice became more anxious, more convincing.

Your mother is not well. She wants to see you.

Is she at your house?

Can you hear her? She's pacing my kitchen. Blanca is trying to calm her but you need to be here. Vero, over and over she cries for her baby. Can you not hear her? Listen, listen Vero.

And then Veronica heard the voice of the woman she was trying to push out of her life. Her mother's cries sent shivers through her torso.

The voice was hysterical.

Veronica could taste tears.

My baby, mommy is sorry. Mommy so sorry my baby mi little Clemente. Oh mijo …

Do you hear her Vero?

I do.

You come see your mother Vero.

Okay, okay.

Veronica looked over at Sabrina, her daughter's head deep in the warm jersey pillowcase.

Sabrina, you're going to meet your nana today.

She made her way to the shower losing the extra large #20 Detroit Lions jersey and her panties along the way. The sting of the water felt good hitting her body and helped to soothe the anxiety escalating in her throat about seeing her mother. Veronica removed the showerhead from its holder and let the warm water drench the inside of her thighs until she could breathe again.

- J U L I U S -

On Sunday morning Julius woke before Grace and Joey. The night before was awkward for him. He and Grace did their best to explain to Joey that mommy and daddy loved him and even still loved each other too but it would be best if daddy and mommy live in different houses. Julius kept quiet for most of the talk with Joey. He admired the tact that Grace used, how she seemed to find all the right words. While Grace talked Julius felt bolts of guilt and shame move through him. He looked at Grace and was amazed at her strength.

When Julius looked at Joey during last evening's talk, he silently promised his son that he would shed the demons in his life; he would heal. Joey sat quietly while his parents talked. After Julius read book number three to Joey and said goodnight, Joey asked him if he would be home in the morning.

I'll be here Joey.

Okay dad.

I'm with you son. I love you.

Love you too.

Good night, son.

The house was quiet. Julius sat up on the couch in the family room. He grabbed the heavy blanket and neatly folded it before placing it on the ottoman. Dressed in black cotton sweatpants and a Luther College T-shirt, Julius walked into the kitchen. He removed the cordless phone from its base. He paused for a moment to let his eyes settle on two tiny swallows perched on top of the fence in the backyard. He opened the sliding glass door and listened to their chirping.

Beauty all around us.

Then he pushed the numbers to call Jessica.

Good morning. Hello?

Hey Jess.

Julius.

I'm surprised you're up so damn early.

Church day baby, church day, come on now. I would ask you to join me but I know some of us don't believe in God. What's up little brother?

Can you help me find Eileen?

Julius we don't have to find mom, I know where she is. You really want to see her? You sure about that?

Not really but I need to.

Julius, like I said, I know where she is.

Right, she's probably in Bluechester right? I have no idea where and I was thinking maybe you did.

And I do. I don't know how happy she'll be on seeing you. There's so much unsaid between you two.

Jess, I'm not going because I miss her and want to give

her a big fucking bear hug. I just need to do some healing.
I need to see her. Will you go with me to see her?

When did you want to go?

I can pick you up at 9.

Damnit, Julius.

What?

You're gonna make me miss my service.

Your service?

Church Julius! Come on bru.

See you at 9?

See you at 9.

Julius clicked the off button on the phone and then
tapped in Lyle's cell phone number. Lyle was always
up early on Sunday mornings during the NFL season.
Sunday mornings for Lyle meant a run of at least eight
miles, sometimes more. After his run he came back home,
showered and took Stacy out to breakfast. At 10 AM
Lyle dug himself into his favorite chair, an old maroon
recliner in his den, to watch football. This was one of
Lyle's Sunday rituals.

Julius!

My man Lyle. What's up?

Just got my eight miles in. I'm about to take my queen
to breakfast and then you know what I do. Game day
baby! How are you?

You know Lyle ... I'm getting through. Grace and I
are going to get a divorce but I think it's going to be
alright.

I'm here for you if you need anything. And I'm sorry Julius. Whatever Stacy and I can do for you or Grace, please man, let us know. How's Joey doing?

He's alright but it's going to be hard. I was calling you to see if I can get that number you had for that therapist.

Let me get it for you.

After Julius ended his conversation with Lyle, he felt a biting twinge tingle his hands.

Demons be gone. He repeated it over and over in his head. *Demons be gone.*

He decided he would prepare breakfast for Grace and Joey and then go see his mother.

- V E R O N I C A -

Where are we going again mommy?

You remember Uncle Roman don't you?

Oh and Aunt Blanca? We're going to their house?

That's where we're going Sabrina. And mommy's mommy will be at the house too. Your nana.

My nana?

Veronica was having second thoughts about taking Sabrina with her. But Sunday was their day to hang out together. On Sunday mornings Veronica would wake up Sabrina and ask her *what be your wish today my princess?* From the conversation with her uncle and hearing her mother in the background, Veronica expected the worst. She could have left Sabrina with Lucy or Inez, yet it just felt right to take her daughter along with her today.

Your nana, girl. This will be the first time you get to see her in person.

Is she nice?

The motion of the car felt soothing under Veronica. She stared at the road in front of her. Image after image of her mother swam in her mind. She stayed in the slow lane; she was in no hurry to reach Bluechester.

Mommy, is she nice?

Is sheeeee nice?

Sabrina looked confused.

Well … yes … she's nice.

Good. I like nice people.

Veronica looked over her right shoulder at Sabrina, comfortably seated in the backseat.

She was glad of the decision she made to keep her daughter.

Uncle Roman:

Veronica you're barely sixteen. How in God's name are you going to raise a baby? No, no too young too young.

Aunt Blanca:

You have the baby and then think at least think about giving the baby a chance to be somebody. You really got yourself into a mess now Veronica.

Veronica had contacted Planned Parenthood to ask about giving her baby up to a family that could care for her soon-to-be newborn. The man on the phone asked her to come down to the office the next day to talk about all of her options. Veronica never went.

You know what Sabrina?

What?

I like nice people too.

Veronica smiled at Sabrina.

You look pretty mommy.

Sabrina grabbed one of the books she brought along for the car ride and began to read.

Veronica tilted the rearview mirror down slightly so she could see her daughter.

Thank you Sabrina.

Veronica raised the rearview mirror back up and loved the fresh taste her tears brought into her mouth.

- J U L I U S -

By the time Julius picked up Jessica and the two of them embarked on the hour and a half drive to Bluechester it was approaching 10 AM.

Sorry I was late Jess. I kinda got a lot going on at the home front.

You know you seem a little um um ... hmm ... I don't know Julius, something. How's the family?

That's a good question.

Julius why do you insist on driving this old ass car? What is it a Festiva or something when you have that nice Chrysler sitting up at the house and what does Grace drive now?

It's a Fiesta. Grace is still driving around in her Honda.

Yeah the Honda, that's a nice car. This bucket you're driving is shit. And you still didn't answer my first question.

Grace and I are getting divorced.

What happened?

A lot.

Julius turned the volume down on the radio. *You like this music Julius* were the first words out of Jessica's mouth when Julius started the engine and pushed in the cassette.

Who is this? Oh wait here's the case… The Cranberries. Okay Julius. Okay now I'm a little concerned.

See Jess, you know how you always say to get things out in the open, right? Like letting go of all the shit that messes with you. I think you even said that you got to let that shit out, right?

Something like that.

Okay, so a lot of the things, the shit I keep in and the way I keep it locked in, I guess more of the way I keep it in doesn't work really well when you're married. The way I cope with my demons …

What demons you got Julius?

Hold on. Shit, if you knew Jess, shit if you knew how many. But you know I get through. I'm getting through each day. Shit though, I'm tired of trying to keep the demons down. It got to a point in my marriage, got to a point where Grace was done with it and done with me. Even better though is that I, I think for the first time, I really believe myself this time, I'm tired of living like I'm living. So a lot has happened. Grace and I, well I love her. Just too much of my own shit gets in the way.

That's it. I see it now, you seem lighter Julius you seem a little … and I know you, well shit you seem lighter in your spirit. You know I read in O that sometimes leaving a marriage can actually begin to heal the couple, something like starting a personal journey into yourself or something like that anyway.

O?

It's a magazine. Oprah's magazine … hello?

Oh. I ain't happy Jess. I'm not healed either.

Hey Julius, seriously though, it's good to see you open up a little.

Julius tussled in his head with the idea of telling his sister what he really wanted to say to her.

How would she take it? Maybe it was best to just let it go. Did she even remember? Did she care?

What he wanted to tell his sister was merely one of the incisions boiling in his chest. An image that crept into his head during his weakest moments. An image so powerful it woke him up at night. An image that he tried to drown on the bellies of prostitutes. It never left him. Maybe it never would. But Jessica had told him to open up. Told him to get things out into the clear.

Brother and sister sat in the small bucket seats and rolled with the Fiesta toward Bluechester. The Cranberries the only sound until Julius mustered up the courage in himself to begin the chipping away of his shame.

Jess.

Julius.

I was awake.

Jessica heard her brother's words and knew exactly what they meant.

Jess, I was awake and I'm sorry that I did nothing to protect you. I was awake, Jess.

You were only nine Julius.

And you were only ten.

- V E R O N I C A -

When Veronica lived in Bluechester she liked how the city always felt at peace on Sundays.

As she drove the final few miles to her uncle's house, she hoped she would gather up the strength to be strong in the face of her mother. Until this morning, it had been more than seven years since she had heard her mother say the name Clemente. And hearing her mother use that name meant that she had to go see her.

When she turned onto her uncle's street, she was once again the scared sixteen-year-old girl who knocked on his door and asked for a place to stay. That was almost eight years ago.

Everything looked the same to her when she saw the house. The leaves of the large weeping willow still draped over the small front yard. The winding flagstone path leading towards the front door was still framed with colorful annuals. Uncle Roman's broken-down Fiat still sat covered in the driveway.

You'll see, I'm going to get that puppy running again one day is what he told Veronica when she teased him about storing dead cars in front of the house.

And Aunt Blanca's prized rose bushes looked just as

alive as they had eight years ago, with yellow, red, and pink roses all unfolded and on display.

Veronica parked the Mustang along side the curb in front of the house.

We made it Sabrina. You ready?

Ready.

Get yourself together girl. Be yourself now okay now I can do this I can do this today eh? I'm okay I'm okay let's go up in here let me go up in here with some calmness some love. Let's hope she is not wasted not high not ... whew ... let me go in here and be helpful I can see this woman I can see her ... she's not me she made me but she's not me okay girl okay now ...

Okay Sabrina. I'm ready too.

- J U L I U S -

Telling Jessica he was sorry made Julius feel as if a tiny layer of rot was able to break its way free and find its way out of the stickem inside his chest.

He decided he would just drive. Let Jessica break the silence when she was ready. They still had at least another forty minutes until they would reach Bluechester. He allowed his thoughts the freedom to roam within him.

Hoped Joey and Grace enjoyed breakfast. They seemed to anyway. Still somewhat awkward but it will be for a while. Mom was a prostitute. Jessica was a prostitute. Found my soothing escape with prostitutes. I'm really getting divorced? Keep working with the demons. So much shit to work through. Turn the car around. I don't want to see her. Got to see her. Start. Need to find a place to live.

What other kind of music do you have up in this Fiesta?

Jessica's voice sounded like it was miles away.

Julius ... other music?

Check under your seat. There should be a red case with some tapes in it.

You need to get you some CDs Julius. And if you insist on driving this raggedy-ass car, at least get you a

CD player.

I like how my cassettes sound.

You just cheap that's all.

You think I make big bank working as a teacher?

I know you make enough to buy you some damn CDs.

Julius cracked a smile. Jessica could always bring his smile out.

Let's see what you got in here. No, no, no, no, no, AC/DC, okay I'll forgive you for having that one, no … Julius, I didn't know you liked the Bee Gees.

I like *Saturday Night Fever*.

Naw, you like them Bee Gees too, huh? Oh now here we go.

Jessica ejected the Cranberries cassette and pushed in Keith Sweat.

Now we can groove.

Jessica played with the fast forward button until she found the song she wanted to hear.

Then she turned up the volume.

Come on J. Make it last forever … all all all … make it last forever and ever … come on tell me now boy that you'll never leave me baby tell me that you always stay will stay with me … make it last now here and forever and ever …

Julius laughed out loud.

Damn, at least get the words right Jess.

Julius let Jessica finish her karaoke session before he ribbed her a little more.

Jess, you still can't sing.

Yeah, but I sing with some heart, don't I?

Whatever. But it still sounds like you're singing inside of a tiny cave with your voice bouncing off the walls and back upside your head.

Funny Julius.

Turn my radio off. Turn it off!

Jessica cranked up the volume louder.

Wait, I want to hear *I wanta her ... I want that girl ...*

No more, No mas, No more sangee for Jess.

Keeping his left hand on the wheel, he looked over at his sister extending his right index finger toward her. His smile bubbling, giddy.

You, Ms. Fiesta, no Sangee Diva. You can't sing. For the safety of the driver, please cease all sound coming from your big mouth.

Jessica sung louder positioning herself in her seat closer to Julius. In between her musical celebration she smiled, letting her tongue fill in the empty space vacated by one of her front teeth. Then she turned off the radio.

I'm about to go free flow on you.

Oh shit, no you don't Jess.

Julius grabbed the wheel with both hands.

Let me brace myself for this.

Jessica put both of her hands over her heart.

Listen.

No, don't you do it.

I sing from my heart letting my spirit roam I come

strong like ...

Noooooo ... stop Jess ...

So you think this woman this woman here is down and out oh noooooo ... I'm back back on my feet again and I'm booming through the fog bringing the fire I'm bringing the love, love, love I'm bringing lots of, check this out now, Julius ... I'm bringing love to the ones who need it I'm bringing love to the sickness all up in me I'm bringing a whole lot of love can you feel it coming through me can you feel it running along inside me can you catch it coming to you so tell me you can feel cause I really got a whole lot of love coming for you watch it pour out of me let me see you glide with its flow come on now baby hmm, hmm, hmm come on Julius, sing with me come on ...

Julius shook his head. He smiled and laughed.

Jess, that really sucked. What the fuck was that?

Yet, he could feel her energy, the song from her heart moving him and despite his reality, her voice was comforting.

-VERONICA-

Uncle Roman looked the same to Veronica. He stood barely 5'2". *I'm 5'5"* is what he told people. His height bothered him to the point of embarrassment at times.

Blanca, do you have to wear those heels tonight?

Oh no mi amor, and Blanca, on many occasions, traded her sexy heels for boring flats.

He wore a pair of loose fit blue jeans, a new pair of white canvas converse high tops, and a white Oakland A's hooded sweatshirt. He looked fit until one got a good look at his midsection. All of the weight on his small body frame settled there. His gut bulged out and hung over his waistline.

Too much Taco Bell Roman.

You know I can work this off anytime I choose to Blanca.

Vero! Blanca, it's Veronica.

Hi Tío.

And look at you mija.

Sabrina smiled.

Come in, come on in. Blanca, Vero is here and come see how big Sabrina is getting. Your mother is asleep in the back bedroom. I'm glad you came, Vero.

Veronica let a soft smile take her face.

Blanca emerged from a swinging door making her way out of the kitchen and into the living room where Veronica, Sabrina, and her husband were standing.

Sit, sit.

Blanca, in her late forties, looked older. Thin to the point where her girlfriends at church talked amongst themselves about her possibly *having that disease, you know that bulimia or that anorexia, not good for her* they would gossip. Blanca sported a green polyester Adidas sweat suit with a dark gray stripe down the outer sides of each pant leg and the sleeves of the jacket. On her feet she wore a pair of pink slip-on house slippers. Her hair, which reached down to the center of her back, was held tightly in a ponytail by three red rubber bands.

Vero, I see you made it.

Blanca then looked at Sabrina.

And look at you. My goodness, oh my goodness look at you. You must be what five, six now?

I'm seven.

Oh my goodness. The years go so fast. They go so fast. Let me give you a hug.

Blanca embraced Sabrina and then hugged Veronica.

Sit, sit you know you are at home here in this house.

Veronica always thought her Aunt Blanca never really meant what she said. That just underneath her kindness was the unspoken. That what her Aunt really wanted to say was *I'll put up with you but I can't wait for you to get your ass out of my house.* Veronica knew it was her uncle who was solely responsible for opening up their house to her when she ran away from her mother. Back then Blanca tolerated her. She pretended to be at peace with her living in their home.

The day Veronica found out she was pregnant Blanca asked her *Ha! So now what are you going to do with a baby?* Veronica looked her Aunt in the eye and said *I don't know, but how come you could never have one, eh?*

The conversation ended.

I have some water on for some tea.

Thank you, Tia.

Sabrina, how about you? What would you like to drink mija? We have some orange juice or um ...

Juice is fine, thank you.

Roman?

Get me some of that orange punch, please.

Orange juice, Roman, orange juice.

Blanca excused herself into the kitchen.

That woman is going to drive me loco. You know what loco means Sabrina? Sabrina smiled shyly. Loco, loco I tell you.

How long has she been asleep for?

After I talked to you, your mother seemed to relax some. I told her you were coming to see her, that you were on the way. Blanca made her a little something to eat trying to calm her nerves. Vero, you should have seen her. Never have I seen her so hysterical and I've seen her boozed up and talking in circles, but this gee whiz. She arrives at my door this morning all ... Roman, sitting in a lazy boy chair across from Veronica and Sabrina, who were sitting on a couch draped with a quilt spotted with pink roses on it, looked at Sabrina and considered his words ... boozed up asking for you. So I called you. She laid down about an hour or so ago. I say let her sleep it off. When she wakes up I guess you two will talk. I'm in the dark here but with you here maybe you can help your mother somehow. She wants you.

Blanca returned from the kitchen carrying two glasses of orange juice in one hand and two cups of hot tea in the other.

Here, take one Roman.

She then made her way to Sabrina. Three feet away from Sabrina she prepared to hand her the other glass of orange juice.

This is for my mija fuck, fuck! Shit Shit Shit Hot Hot Hot Oh Shit!

The two cups of tea slipped out from under Blanca's grip and fell to the floor. Boiled water spilled on Blanca's hands, arms, and made its way down the front of her sweatsuit.

Blanca, you try to be superwoman. See what happens! And don't swear in front of Sabrina. Get ahold of yourself

Blanca.

Blanca glared at Roman.

Let me get some towels and clean up this mess.

You do that Blanca, por favor. My wife, I don't know about you sometimes.

- J U L I U S -

So why is it so important for you to see mom today?

Which exit Jess?

Lantern Street. Go west. You getting a divorce must have something to do with it. I still can't believe you and Grace are splitting up. Maybe you two will be able to work it out down the road somewhere.

Not going to happen Jess. I have to heal or I'll just …

Just what?

What?

You were saying or I'll just … something you were going to say.

Well, just stay fucked up.

Oh.

There's Lantern.

Julius turned the car's right blinker on and moved from the center lane of the freeway over to the right lane. He battled with the voices inside his head.

You're fucked up You really are fucked up.

He tried to focus all of the energy moving inside him toward the voices. He wanted to squash the sound.

The place we're going to is where mom has been living for a few months. We usually talk at least once a week. I

164

didn't talk with her last week because, well anyway, after we talked this morning I called the number she's at and the phone was cut off, again. You know her though.

Who is she staying with?

Take the west exit Julius. Some friend of hers she met in church. They live in a little apartment downtown. Go right here. Follow this street for a while. This will take us downtown.

After a few minutes of silence, Jessica poked her brother in the ribs.

Hey!

You're getting quiet on me J. Plus, you never answered my question. You nervous?

He knew which question he had not answered but he played like he didn't.

You asked me a lot of damn questions. Which one?

I'm not going to push you on it. I hope this is a good idea you going to see mom.

Do I keep straight? We've been on this street for a while. You sure you know where you're going?

Somebody is a little nervous. Hearing it in your voice. Keep straight. I'll let you know when it's time to turn. Actually, we are getting pretty close. I've only been there one time myself.

You sure you know where it is?

Sure do.

She probably won't even be there.

I don't know Julius. Church is out by now and she usually spends Sundays cooking up a big dinner with her friend. She'll be there.

You know Jess, I haven't seen her, damn, since …

Since she embarrassed your ass on Thanksgiving at Grace's parents, right? That was more than seven years ago.

The memory of that afternoon, still alive, scrolled across Julius' eyes.

Yep, I guess so, about eight years ago. I don't think I have even talked to her, what, maybe two or three times in those eight years.

Turn right up at this next street. It should be Baxter, oh no wait, here it is, it's Buxter. Now I should be able to recognize the building. We're real close now.

Buxter Street was tucked off the main hub of downtown Bluechester. It ran parallel, four blocks from Templeton, one of the main downtown streets. It was Sunday, approaching noon, and the street was quiet. Many of the window shops lining the street were closed. Wide concrete sidewalks, with leafless trees planted every fifteen feet or so, bordered the bumpy street.

Slow down a bit J. Let me see here. No, keep going a little further. It should be coming up here real soon now. Keep going a little bit more.

Julius placed his left hand on his left thigh trying to stop it from twitching.

There it is.

Where?

We passed it. That blue building back there. Go to the stoplight up there and flip a U.

Jess, I can't, we're on a one-way street.

Well just go back, go around or something. Figure it out or something. Damn.

You nervous too Jess?

-VERONICA-

It had almost been two hours since Veronica arrived at her uncle's house.

Uncle Roman took Sabrina with him to pick up lunch at Taco Bell. While they were away, Blanca stayed in the kitchen, *I'm just going to make myself some Cup of Noodle, I don't eat fast food,* leaving Veronica sitting in the living room waiting for her mother to wake up.

Uncle Roman and Sabrina came in the house giggling.

Mommy, Uncle Roman is silly.

You don't know how silly I am mija.

He removed the two straws sticking out of his nostrils.

We better toss these out mija.

What'd you get sweetheart?

One tostada, some cinnamon twists, and root beer.

Tell her mija. Tell her what Tio said to try.

The snorting laugh coming from her uncle was hilarious.

Wait, give me a napkin from the bag mija, this is too funny. I'm making myself cry here. Mija, please napkin por favor.

Did Tio play one of his tricks on you Sabrina?

Tell her mija.

Sabrina, feeding off of Uncle's Roman's contagious laughter, began laughing again herself.

When we ordered our food Uncle Roman said I should try an um ... a ...

Bell Beefer Burger, mija. A Bell Beefer Burger.

Veronica caught the giggles too.

Tio, now you know they stopped making Bell Beefers a long time ago.

I know, but you should have seen the look on the kid, poor little guy, behind the counter. He had to call up a manager and then the eighteen-year-old manager was just as confused as he was. They had never heard of it. So I acted all upset saying my niece is here visiting me from Guadalajara and I promised her a Bell Beefer.

You are a fool, Tio.

But wait, then, Sabrina and I are at the counter with three or four Taco Bell employees huddled up looking up at their own menu. *We don't see a Bell Beefer up there sir.* So I say don't sweat it but you should know your Taco Bell history. And I told them all about the delicious Bell Beefer.

You have really lost your mind Tio.

Oh it was fun though and your daughter played the part so well. She looked all serious, like *I really want my Bell Beefer*. It was a hoot hey mija?

Sabrina was still laughing.

What's so funny Roman? Blanca walked into the

living room with a cup of soup. Still giddy, Roman looked at his wife.

That's not hot is it Blanca? Careful with that.

Blanca tried her best to laugh off her husband's words.

Well let's eat. We got you a couple of tostadas Vero. I remember that was your favorite.

You remembered right.

You're missing out Blanca. Damn, I love the Bell. And she eats soup.

My soup is fine. Veronica how much longer do you think your mother will sleep?

I don't know …

Well, she's been in there for a while. I checked on her. Looked to me like she's out for the night.

When we finish up this good food here, if she's not up yet, I'll wake her and let her know that Vero is here. You and Sabrina probably have better things to do than to sit up in this house all afternoon. She'll appreciate being woken up to see you Vero.

Veronica smiled softly at her Tio.

- JULIUS -

Park at that meter right there.

Hold on Jess, let me …

You're going to have to parallel park it.

I see a spot up there. It'll be easier to get into.

Take it then. Now Julius, promise me when we get up in the apartment you're going to be alright, you're going to be cool.

What do you mean by that?

I'm just saying, you waking up this morning needing to see her, see her today, there must something heavy on you. Just don't go up in here bringing up things that are hurtful. She's trying to get her life together and I don't know, you coming back into her life … shoot, I don't know.

Julius parked the car and pulled up the emergency brake.

I'm really happy to hear that. I can't promise you anything. Thanks for bringing me here to see her, if she is up there in that building. I've come here to speak my truth to her and I hope she's able to speak a little truth to me too. I didn't come here to hurt anyone.

I'm just saying to be easy, take it slow.

Jess, you are too much.

And you love me.

I don't know sis. You're damn hard to love.

Me? You know that's not true. Now stop playing. I love you bru. So just … just say what you have to but no broken hearts. Too many of those around here.

The apartment complex, sprayed with sky-blue paint, looked more like a hotel to Julius. There was a small lobby area which housed slender, gold metal mailboxes for the residents. A couple of small wooden tables with chairs rested in the center of the lobby. A large cork bulletin board, hung off center on one wall, was tacked with flyers and business cards. Julius and Jessica made their way to the elevator just to the right of the bulletin board. While waiting for the elevator to make its way down, Julius surveyed the lobby.

You smell that?

Smell what?

Funk, Jess, funk.

Must be the laundry room over there.

Julius spotted a door next to the mailboxes. He could hear the rhythmic bustling of a dryer.

Goddamn, somebody close the door.

Hit number five.

Number five. Done. Think she'll be here? Jess?

Hold on, I got a cramp in my toe.

What the hell?

Hold on damnit!

As the elevator slowly made its way upward, Jessica removed the cream pump from her left foot, lifted her leg in the air and began to flex her foot back and forth while trying to maintain her balance in the moving elevator.

What in the hell, Jess?

Gotta a cramp, shit, come on pop, pop. Ohhhh … there we go. Whew, man.

Julius looked at his sister.

You're funny as hell. You should have seen yourself.

Had to work that cramp out. And yeah, she'll be here.

Sounds more like toe jam to me.

Whatever. Come on.

Julius followed Jessica out of the elevator into a dimly lit hallway. Beige doors, identified by a letter and number stuck just under the doors' peepholes, lined the musty hallway.

You know which one it is?

D89.

Jessica continued her march down the hallway. Julius slowed his pace trying to gather himself.

A part of him hoped his mother wouldn't be there. He had no idea how he would say what he planned to say. *Maybe Jessica was right. Why bring up the past? Let it go. Fuck it, I have to know where I come from. Stop these motherfuckn' worms and shit.*

He could feel the worms again inching their way through his bloodstream, making a path to his heart and brain, where they rested for the gnawing. He hoped his mother could provide the answers that would kill the invaders, stop their reaping of his flesh.

The voices returned:

Turn around Julius
turn around
 you don't want to see her
 pick your ass up
 poor me somebody help me
 momma help me
 give me the answers

 you are fucking pathetic you weak ass man

 help me deal with the demons
 the worms are going to get me give me the answers momma
tell me why

 all your weak ass questions

 leave her be no no talk with her find out the truth help ease
this loneliness
 no hurt to her intended
 just the truth

You got a little mumble going on back there Julius.

Julius, embarrassed, picked up his pace.

Just gathering my thoughts.

Jessica grabbed her brother's hand.

It's alright Julius. I talk to myself sometimes too.

Holding her brother's cold hand and now standing in front of door D89, Jessica wondered why she felt like she was ten years old again.

We made it ... someone is here too. You hear the music?

She pounded on the door.

Dang Jess, easy.

You hear that music?

I know but that was a loud ass knock. You trying to beat the door in? Damn. Hey, what's her friend's name?

East.

What?

Stop laughin'. That's her name.

East? What the fuck?

Julius, focus yourself now.

And her last name is West right?

Mom said she changed her name to signify some miracle.

The woman opened the door and stood in complete silence trying to recognize the two people standing in front of her. She was dressed in her best church clothes. The hem of her beautiful burgundy dress rested just below her knees. She wore white nylons. Julius noticed a little run in the nylons just above her right ankle. She wore no shoes and her hair was pressed neatly back into a bun. Julius surmised she was in her early sixties like his mother.

Hi, East.

Oh okay, okay! Jessica. How you doin' young lady? Come on in darling.

This is my brother, Julius. Julius this is East.

This is Julius? Let me get your mother. Eileen, come on out here girl. Eileen? Julius it's nice to meet you. This is going to be a real surprise for her on this beautiful Sunday. Eileen! Eileen! You better come on out here.

- K A T R I N A -

After he finished his fifth taco, Roman made the short walk to the back of his house. He slowly moved down the narrow hallway past doors opening to a bathroom, an office, and his and Blanca's bedroom. At the end of the hall, to his left, he looked at the closed door leading into the back bedroom. He imagined his sister sprawled out on top of the bed. He wished they were a lot closer.

Hey Katrina? Katrina, you awake there? Katrina?

Roman moved closer to the bed. The room was nearly dark. Splashes of gold sprayed out of each side of the white window shade. A queen-size bed sat smack in the center of the room. Katrina's left hand draped over one side of the bed a foot or so away from touching the window. Earlier she had kicked the quilt off her. It lay at the end of the bed. The way it gathered there reminded Roman of a king cobra.

Katrina lay on her stomach. Her body in a tight line like a straight arrow. Her head faced toward the window, away from her brother. Her straight, brown hair covered one side of her face, swooping down over it like a spider fern. She still had on her shoes, black pumps, the heels peeling and scratched. She wore a pair of blue jeans and a red sweater.

Katrina your daughter is here. Right out there in the front room. You asked to see her. And she came.

Roman raised his voice.

Katrina. Are you going to get up?

Katrina opened her eyes. She felt a throbbing between her ears. She thought she still might be drunk. The bed was warm to her. She liked the room's darkness. Even its smell was comforting. She didn't know where it was but she knew there had to be a basket of potpourri somewhere near. She ignored Roman's call to awake. *Did he say Veronica was here?* She wasn't sure.

Roman moved in closer. He lightly touched one of Katrina's shoulder blades.

Katrina, you need to get up and go see your daughter. Sabrina is with her too.

I'm awake.

Good.

Katrina sat up. She could smell the remnants of the morning's vodka on her breath. She ran her tongue over her front teeth letting it gather tiny morsels of plaque. Rubbed her eyes.

She brought Sabrina with her?

That's what I said.

You want to talk with Vero in here first? You let me know what you want to do.

Katrina felt the tears coming again.

How do I face her?

Roman walked around the end of the bed to see Katrina's face. Pulled up the window shade. The room filled with whiteness.

I think you start by actually going to see her out there. You know? Take it from there. You said you need to talk to her, right? You should have seen yourself this morning. You really need to get help with your drinking situation. That's all I got to say. I hope you get up and go see your daughter and your grandbaby. I'm going back out. What do you want to do?

Katrina stood up. Much taller than Roman, she always imagined her father a lot taller than Roman's father, she could see the top of her brother's head.

Mi hermano. You are so theatrical.

I'm serious about your drinking. You trying to kill yourself?

Yes, I think I am, Roman.

Hush Katrina.

Roman turned and started for the door. Katrina followed. She walked so closely behind that Roman could feel her breath brushing up against his neck. Blanca was the first person Katrina saw in the living room.

So I see you weren't passed out for the night.

Blanca looked Katrina over. She found comfort seeing Katrina like this. Hungover, ragged, and beat down. Maybe her existence wasn't so bad, certainly not as bad as *Katrina's fucked up life.*

Katrina ignored Blanca's comment. Roman stepped

away from his sister putting her in full view.

Katrina's hands began to shake. Seated on the couch, she saw two generations, Veronica and Sabrina.

Sabrina moved closer to her mother, grabbing her arm at its bend. Katrina fought back the shame she felt in her stomach. How she hated to be seen like this by her daughter. Veronica rose up off the couch and made her way to where her mother stood. The image of Clemente falling played inside her mind.

She touched her mother's hands to stop the shaking. Saw her mother's red painted toenails strapped inside her scuffed up black heels. No doubt in her mind that she still walked the streets.

Katrina wanted the embrace to go on forever. It was awkward at first. Katrina's body went limp. Veronica kept squeezing.

Hi mommy.

The moisture running down Katrina's face found its way onto Veronica's neck. Veronica let the embrace go.

Mommy, this is Sabrina.

Hi Nana.

Katrina just stared at her granddaughter.

-EILEEN-

East, what's all the ruckus out here about?

Eileen stepped into the small, square living room. She rested her eyes on Jessica first. She thought Jessica looked nice. She liked how her black hair was pulled into a tight ponytail and laid tight on her scalp. Eileen could smell the hair grease.

Hey mom.

The greeting from Jessica went right through Eileen as she turned her attention to the pale redheaded man standing next to her daughter. Eileen wasn't even sure how long it had been since she had last seen her son. There wasn't a day that went by that she didn't think of the day when he was conceived. She could have called him whenever she pleased. She had his phone number but Eileen was never a phone person. She had her son's address too. Each time she thought about writing to him the words never came to fill the paper before the tears moved in. Maybe she had sent a card or two. She wondered. Maybe she hadn't.

Hi Mom. How you been doing lately?

Julius' voice sounded strange to Eileen. Before speaking, Eileen looked her son up and down. He had to be over forty now. Julius wore a pair of clean white leather K-Swiss on his feet. His faded black Levi's softly touched each shoe. Eileen liked the maroon and blue striped polo shirt he had on. She had a hard time looking at his face. She snuck quick peeks. *He's tired. He's stressed. Forehead is all heavy and scrunched.* She didn't know how to respond to her son. Instead she walked the three feet from where she was over to Jessica and hugged her.

Julius put his hands in his pockets and began to rock his body, ever so slightly, to the left and then to the right. He could hear Jessica whisper something into the ear of his mother. He sensed that his mother was crying.

East announced in an excited and loud voice that she was going to go gather up some snacks. She walked toward the kitchen saying I'm going to give you all a little time in here to settle in together.

Eileen and Jessica ended their embrace and Julius could feel his mother's eyes back on him. He looked over at Jessica who smiled at him. Julius decided right there and then that if he ever got a little extra money in the foreseeable future he would give it to Jessica so she could get her a new front tooth.

Mom, we drove down here to see you. It was Julius' idea. You look so good.

I feel good Jessica. I feel good for the first time in a long time let me tell you child.

Looking at her mother, Jessica could tell, as could Julius, that she was clean. There was no hint of alcohol on her.

When was the last time we been together, us three all together like this under the same roof? I couldn't tell you the last time I been in the same room with both of my kids. Yet y'all ain't kids anymore. Lord, give me some strength today. When was the last time?

Eileen moved her eyes from Julius' chest to Jessica for a response. Julius spoke.

It's been seven years at least mom. Thanksgiving seven years ago at Grace's parents place.

Yes, you are right. Seven years, huh?

Seven years.

Eileen was approaching sixty two now and the rough edges of her life were showing. Her belly fought for room under the vinyl red belt fastened around the white dress she wore. Her hair was gray and pretty. Julius noticed how his mother's hair laid wildly on the outer edges of her face and down to the tip of her shoulders in the back. Her cocoa butter skin still glistened.

And how is Grace and your little one?

They're doing alright. Joey is getting big.

Hmm ... you two come on away from the door. We can sit up in here a while. Come on come on over here and let's sit for a while, come.

Mom I came to ...

I know why you come here Julius.

Julius felt a shot of dread shoot through his body.

Please, just come and sit down for a minute.

Julius looked at Jessica who was already seated on a black leather couch that was pushed snug against a red wall. Eileen joined her. A papasan chair, the same deep lush shade of red as the wall, sat in a corner next to the couch. Julius made his way toward it. From where he sat, Julius could see East in the kitchen. He smelled bacon sizzling on the stove. He heard East humming. He liked it. He liked the peacefulness of East. Julius made several attempts to get comfortable in the papasan. Each attempt failed so he finally decided to move himself all the way to the very edge of the chair. Eileen sat on the couch just to the left of him. If he wanted, he could have reached his left hand out and touched his mother's hand that rested on the armrest of the couch.

How was church today mom?

It was fine Jessica, just fine baby.

East poked her head through the rectangle opening in the kitchen that looked into the living room.

I'm making us something to eat. I'm going to give you some time out there. If anyone needs a drink you can get on up in here and help yourself now.

East is good people. She's been good to me. Been real good to me.

Every time his mother said a word she seemed to be on the brink of tears. He thought of the words he planned to say to her next very carefully. He could not say them at all and make this visit *nice to see you mom, hope we can see more of each other in the future.*

Maybe what his mom could tell him would help keep the worms at bay, though. Help kill the worms, stop them from eating him from the inside out. Keep the teeth-bearing worms from defecating on his life.

Julius bit his bottom lip before speaking.

Hey mom, you said you know why I came here. How do you know that?

Well, I don't know the exact reason why you here Julius. But I think I have an idea why you're here. I do know that I have not been truthful with you and there is a time when a child needs to know the truth. So you're here for the truth. Right? The whole ugly damn truth. Is that what you're here for?

Head down. Eyes on his chest. Julius muttered, I'm here for the truth.

Then I need to do some talking. You know Julius, in the past I was in no place to tell you any kind of truth about anything. Remember when you and Jessica went to stay with my sister and that crazy ass man of hers? I'm still very sorry for letting you go that morning. I knew Bobbie was crazy back then. And I am sorry it took me so long to come and get you from them. My sister meant well. Bobbie is just crazy. He's a sick man.

Jessica wrapped an arm around her mother.

Mom, you don't have to keep saying you are sorry.

Oh ... yes I do Jessica. I really do child. But I'll cut to the reason why I think your brother came here. And Julius, if I'm wrong you tell me. I ain't going to be wrong, though.

You want me to just tell you why I'm here?

I know why you're here. And now that I'm older, shit now that I'm clean, I'm able to deal a little better with all the ugliness.

Should I give you and Julius a little privacy?

I don't mind if you stay, Jessica, and East already knows what I'm about to tell your brother.

You want me to stay Julius?

We family Jess, so yeah, stay alright?

Okay.

Eileen flicked her tongue back and forth inside her mouth. She did it so fast that Jessica and Julius could see her cheeks puff out a bit when the tongue hit the soft walls of her inner cheeks.

Jessica asked if her mother was okay.

I'm just trying to gather up my thoughts. Give me a minute.

Then, just as quick as it had started, the movement in her mouth stopped.

Julius, what I'm about to tell you has been in my heart for a long time. It's broken me on several occasions. Maybe the uneasiness of all the evil from it is tearing at you and I suppose it would be because you don't know the truth about your past.

Wait. Mom, before you go into this evil thing about my past …

Julius paused before he completed his words, his eyes

now fixed on the deep brown eyes of his mother.

I just came here to ask you about my father. I just came here with Jessica to get some clarity on who my father is or was or whatever.

Eileen frowned at her son.

Julius, see I'm about to tell you about your father. Umhummm, see I know why you come here and I'm going to tell you the truth. Lord knows I should have told you a long time ago and you know that probably would have helped us both. But I kept that evil right here in my heart. I kept it all right up in here. All of it.

Mom let me get you some tissue.

Hold on Jessica. If I choose to cry you gonna have to let your momma cry. Please, sit down, you need to hear this too. I know you know who your daddy is but your brother don't know his and it's tearing at his heart. My tears can move on me. I'll be fine.

The tears moving down his mother's face made Julius uncomfortable. Yet the evil that his mother was set to tell captured his attention. He could relate to evil.

Worms. The evil I've done to Grace. The evil I'm doing to myself.

Eileen spoke in a quiet tone. As she spoke she looked at Julius. Julius let his head sag toward his chest. He closed his eyes and readied himself.

Your daddy Jessica turned me on to the streets ... wait let me be truthful here, you deserve that. Your daddy Jessica turned me out. In other words I started to sell my body for your daddy. I was young and pretty. He told me this was the way we was going to make some money. All I wanted was to be with your daddy and do my drugs. We had so many drugs. I was numb half the time. Even when I was numb, high, drunk, whatever, I hated having to lay down with some strange man and let him fire into me. I tried two times to leave your father. One time he found me hiding from him at my sister's house. He came up in there and dragged me by the hair from one of the bedrooms all the way to his car. Bobbie, who at the time was just my sister's boyfriend, watched the whole thing and didn't move a bone. Coward. I don't blame him, though. Your daddy would have killed him. The second time I tried to run off to stay with my cousin Rita in Fresno. He tracked me down somehow. When he found me he was so nice. He told me just to get in the car. Told me he wasn't mad at me. Just glad he had found me. When we got back to Bluechester, he fucked me then beat on me. Then he left me in a motel room for a couple of weeks to heal. He would drop in every day to give me some food and some weed. He told me once I healed then it was time to get my ass back out on the street again.

Eileen paused. Tears on her.

What I am telling you is the truth and you should know this.

Julius and Jessica didn't mutter a sound.

I'll keep talking then. I don't blame your daddy Jessica. I mean I've forgiven him for a lot of the things he did to me. I even see him sometimes at the church I attend. He told me he tries to call you when he can. I don't blame him. I was the one who got in the car with him leaving Fresno. I was the one in love with him. Boy, he used me though. But I used him too for drugs. We traded drugs for sex, sex for drugs, beatings for drugs. It was an ugly time in my life. Then it got worse. I stayed in Bluechester with your daddy for another year. That's when you were born. Then one day the police came for him. He told me I better be here when he got back. I left. And that was the end of our relationship. You was just a little baby then. Thought I'd try to go to a community college or something. I still sold my body every now and then. When your daddy got out of jail, he never did come looking for us. I heard on the street that he joined the Nation of Islam and started preaching to folks doing the same things he use to do on the streets. So anyway, I had me a tiny little studio, not far from here actually. You slept with me in my bed. I still walked the streets a couple of nights a week. I enrolled in school, just taking two classes. I felt like I was on the verge of doing something right in my life too. So now ... Julius, what I'm about to tell you right now is all the truth you may want to hear. Maybe by giving it some air you and I can breathe somewhat better today. Well ... the truth is what it is and the truth don't sit up in one's mouth too long for no one, ever. I had a late afternoon class. A Tuesday class. Jessica you were at Miss Mary's house, bless her soul, she's dead now. Hmm ... I left school and decided I would turn three tricks, make some money before it was time to come pick you up later that night. I'll never forget them three tricks that night. The first one was a big country boy from Alabama. He was so nervous. Said he was new to this. You know picking up a hooker. We was through in five minutes. He never even put his little thang in me; he came all over my panties.

Eileen began to laugh. Y'all can laugh too.

Jessica grinned.

Julius bit his lower lip.

That second trick was a sweetie.

East entered the room and sat down on the carpeted floor next to Julius.

You all fine with me here?

East this is your home. We're more than fine.

I know that. Julius are you alright with me here is what I want to know?

Julius loved the vibe coming from East. He felt peace moving from her body.

I'm fine.

East smiled and crossed her legs butterfly style.

So this second trick was real sweet. Looking back now, I think it was God's way of giving me some kindness before the wickedness arrived. That second trick was so sweet. You know I still remember his name or the name he told me was his name. Hmm ... he said my name is Jay and told me I was pretty. He told me you are so pretty over and over again. After Jay paid me, I thought about just going to pick you up Jessica and get on home. I made enough money to hold us over until we got the government check. Then I figured well I'm already out here I'll do just one more. Just as I left the parking lot of the motel that I had just been at with Jay, just as I got to the sidewalk, I saw a man approaching me on a bike. My gut said something ain't right here. He rode his ten-speed by me then circled back. I thought he was a cop. He looked so serious. He asked me how much? He asked me was I into anal sex? Asked me if I could suck a good dick all the way down to the balls? This guy was creepy. I told him, look I don't do no anal mess and that first we need to get a room and then we can go from there. When he went into the motel lobby to pay I had my chance to leave but I didn't trust my instincts back then. I was just a kid. I was barely twenty. I should have left. I had an opening. You want all the details Julius because I'm going to give them to you. The fool brought his bike up into the room. After he laid $50.00 on the night stand by the bed, he asked me if I wanted to share a joint. I told him no told him once I left here I was going to pick up my daughter and I didn't want to be high going to get her. So he smoked the joint. When he climbed on top of me I could smell fresh rum on his lips. He was rough with me. I just wanted him to finish so I could leave. When he finished, he pulled out of me and sprayed his semen all over my face. Told me to enjoy some whiteness. He told me to enjoy some whiteness you black bitch.

He told me just because I am light skinned don't forget I am still a black bitch. Then before I could get my bearings straight he socked me. I don't know how many times he hit me. He hit me in my jaw and eye and told me if I moved he would continue. I screamed hoping someone would hear me. I started to scream again and his fist hit my face again. He put a pillow over my mouth and told me not to say another damn thing until he was through or he would cut me and he showed me a pocket knife that he pulled out from one of his white tube socks. He was naked except for those tube socks and a pair of camel construction boots he kept on his feet. After he took the pillow off my face I told myself to do all I could to get out of here alive. I thought of Connie, one of my girlfriends who nearly died after a trick beat her into a pulp after she refused to give him free seconds of her body. I just wanted to survive. I kept quiet. My face hurt. I felt the blood leaving my face and racing to my neck and shoulders. He came again this time staying inside of me. Then he got up off the bed and I thought it was over. But it wasn't, no, he came back holding a small silver pump, a little slender bike pump. He said get on your belly bitch and put your ass in the air. I rolled onto my belly and when I didn't put my ass in the air he did it for me. Then he stuck the pump in me until he got bored doing that then he stuck himself in me, then the pump again, then himself again. Before he came, he rolled me onto my back and came in both of my eyes. The last thing he said to me was now you can see what a good fuck feels like. I looked at him. His bright red hair. His white skin. He disgusted me. I told him God don't like evil you muthafucka.

Eileen took a deep breath and looked at Julius who was now out of the papasan sitting on the carpet next to East. His eyes closed. His right hand twitching. Jessica stared at her mother. Eileen put her head in her hands.

Julius, that man is your father. Julius, hear me now son. That man is your father and truth be told I can't ever love you. Oh, I tried but I can't. Do you hear me! That man … I'm done talking about that man. I should have had an abortion. Lord knows I should have. Shit. Everybody told me to abort. Abort! That's what they told me. But I don't believe in killin' nobody. That's my truth Julius. That's all I can tell you about your father, the rapist. That's all I got. Shit, that's all I got. I can't love you.

Eileen rose up off the couch and headed toward the kitchen.

-VERONICA-

Mija, you don't want to bring your baby with us?

No, no mommy, Uncle Roman challenged her to a game of Connect Four. It's okay, plus you really wanted to see me. Come on, we'll walk. We'll talk, eh?

Veronica and her mother walked slowly. Their steps in unison, each foot striking the sidewalk leading away from Roman and Blanca's home. Veronica was slightly taller than her mother. As they moved down the sidewalk, on occasion, the two lightly brushed shoulders. Veronica figured that her mother would not begin the conversation that was brewing since the departure of Clemente.

-CLEMENTE-

Clemente was an undersized baby. When he was born he weighed barely four pounds and was thirty-two days earlier than expected. The day Katrina took Clemente home from the county hospital was the day that Veronica turned thirteen.

Meet your baby brother.

Veronica thought he was so tiny. She thought he was so pretty too. His little fingers. All that black hair on his head. His small arms. His skinny legs. Veronica instantly fell in love with Clemente.

Mommy he's so pretty.

He really is mija.

During the first couple of months of Clemente being home Veronica noticed a big shift in her mother. Veronica was happy to see that her mother drank less. The different men who frequented the house in the evenings lessened too. Veronica loved listening to her mother hum to Clemente. She always told Veronica that Clemente was a good baby. Then one day when Veronica arrived home from school she noticed that Clemente was asleep on top of her mother's bed and her mother was not home.

She waited.

Just before 10 PM her mother returned home.

Mommy what happened? You were gone when I got home

from school. Clemente was home by himself.

Well … I knew you were coming home and I had to go out for a while.

Veronica felt tears gathering. She smelled the alcohol leaving her mother's mouth.

Where is he? Did you give him the bottle in the fridge? I left you a note didn't I?

I didn't find a note Mommy. I fed him. He's sleeping in his playpen. He's right there.

Oh, good.

Her mother grabbed the large hand of the man she entered the house with. As they made their way to the bedroom the man used his free hand to slap the ass of Veronica's mother. During the night, Veronica was awakened by Clemente two times. The first time she thought he was hungry so she fed him a bottle of Similac and he settled himself back to sleep. The second time she changed his diaper and laid him back down in the playpen. Clemente cried. Veronica prepared another bottle for him.

Clemente cried. Veronica held him. She rocked him and finally he fell back to sleep in her arms.

Veronica stayed home from school the next day. She was dressed and ready to go to school but when she went to tell her mother she was leaving she knew she couldn't leave Clemente. Her mother was asleep. The man who was with her last night was gone. A two liter of Coke, nearly empty, and an empty bottle of rum sat on the floor beside the bed. A used condom was stuffed into the rum bottle.

It was nearly 11 AM when Katrina made her way out of the bedroom. She walked by Veronica and Clemente making her way to the refrigerator where she grabbed a watermelon-flavored wine cooler.

Vero, thanks for taking care of your brother last night. You can go on to school now.

Veronica stood still. She held Clemente in her arms.

You need lunch money? Here, give me Clemente so you can go.

Veronica handed Clemente to her mother.

I can't go to school now.

Why?

Mommy the day is half over. It's embarrassing to go to school this late.

Mañana then. You want to come outside with me? I need some fresh air.

Mommy let me hold him.

I'm not drunk Vero.

Veronica saw it happen. Her mother's bare foot missing the step, losing her balance as she left the entrance of the house. She saw the slow fall forward. She watched her mother pull Clemente tightly into her chest. Veronica braced herself before her mother hit the concrete of the front porch. She heard the thud of her mother's head hitting the concrete. Veronica looked for Clemente before realizing that he was trapped under their mother. Katrina turned her head to look back and up at Veronica. Veronica could now see the blood escaping from underneath her mother's body. Her mother's weight too much for Clemente to bear.

- V E R O N I C A -

Tell me Mommy, what does your life look like these days? Uncle Roman said you cry for your baby. I do too but not as often as I used to. But I cry for Clemente too. What do your days look like Mommy?

Vero, I'll be fifty before I know it. I'm still working the streets. I don't have much, only my body to support me and it won't last forever. I have a little room that I rent by the week. It's just a motel room. When you went off and I'm glad you did, my days didn't change. I did the same things. Meet a man to get some money and he gets to sleep with me in exchange. I'm tired. I'm tired. And oh Veronica, your daughter, she is so beautiful. I'm so proud of you.

As her mother talked, Veronica thought about how similar their lives were. She was thankful that she and Sabrina lived in a nice home and that the tricks she turned were a little more upscale than the ones her mother was turning out there on the streets. However, with the exception of her mother's drinking, their lives shared many similarities.

I told your uncle to call you. I can't live with the memory. He would be ten tomorrow. I killed my baby.

Veronica stopped walking. She turned toward her mother.

Mommy, hear me now, eh? Now don't tell me you killed Clemente. Accident. It was. That's what it was.

No, Vero. I did kill my baby. I crushed him. I heard the snap of his neck. I heard the breaking of his skull.

Veronica wiped the tears in her eyes with the sleeve of her shirt.

I did too mommy. I did too. You tripped coming out of the door. That's all. If the thought of you being drunk or hung over when it happened is haunting you, then do something about that but don't tell me you killed Clemente. It was an accident. The court said it was an accident. The court did not say you killed him. I don't want to hear it.

I don't need the court to tell me what happened that day. I killed my baby. You can call it an accident, whatever. I know. I know that Clemente is not here with me because I was not sober. I was too busy … well, I'm just one hopeless lady.

Mommy, listen to me. You can replay the story of Clemente in your mind until it kills you too or you can understand that you are still alive. See that's it. You are still alive. You have the time to make a new life for yourself. I still see Clemente in my head. I still see him too. I was there mommy, don't forget that.

What am I'm supposed to do when I dream of him? What? All the shame mija. All the guilt.

Veronica thought of what her mother always told her to do when things were rough, when life was throwing bricks of shit at you. She remembered how her mother would calmly tell her to cope, *you have to just learn to cope with what is front of you.*

You didn't kill him. And even if you had it was not intentional. You fell. He fell with you.

I'm not going to make it Veronica. I see him everywhere. The drinking doesn't even soothe me like it used to before. I'm falling apart. I thought I was so strong, no ... I'm not the strong one. My little girl, you are the strong one. You hear me don't you? All the years I was half-there for you. Half-drunk. All them men at the house. I'm so ashamed.

That's all in the past. You know all that stuff is back in the past. You were doing the best you could do at the time. I would look at you when you were drinking and wait for you to be you again. Even then I knew if you could have done differently or done better you would have.

I didn't though. Really, Veronica, I really didn't do the best I knew I could do. I didn't actually do shit.

Part Four
TOO MANY DEMONS

Mama, take this badge off of me
I can't use it anymore
It's gettin' dark, too dark for me to see
I feel like I'm knockin' on heaven's door

Knockin' on Heaven's Door

- Bob Dylan

- J U L I U S -

Julius glanced at the alarm clock on the nightstand. 12:08 AM.

After he dropped off Jessica, seven hours earlier, he found his way to the Prime Gentlemen's Club, which was just around the corner from Jessica's apartment complex. Having heard his mother rattle out the truth of his existence ignited his body, a fretfulness that only could be deadened by the intoxicating softness of a woman.

Inside the strip club, he found this gentleness sitting under a woman named Kelly.

As Kelly danced on his lap, up and down and side to side in beat with the music of Tupac filling the small club, Julius wished he could eat up her pretty pink flesh like the worms he felt nibbling at him inside his chest.

Before he even said his goodbyes to Jessica, before his mother even walked him and Jessica to the door, Julius knew where he was headed once he was alone. There would be no phone call to check in with Grace or Joey. There would be no call to Lyle. There would be no call to anyone.

Julius would do what he did best. Lose himself into the

night under and over the bellies of women who he paid for the opportunity to silence the emptiness tormenting his existence.

When he made his way out of the gentlemen's club, Julius drove his Fiesta out of the parking lot and to the Cloud 9 motel directly across the street. A college student closed his accounting book to check him in.

12:08 AM. Julius paced the room.

He had $120 dollars in cash and he still had his Visa card, the one that he secured for himself without Grace knowing. He made the minimum payment on it monthly. Each month when he received the bill, online and delivered to his email account, he was ashamed. There was a balance of more than $8,000 on the card.

12:10 AM.

Julius reached into the back left pocket of his jeans and pulled out his wallet. Behind his California drivers license and his Safeway club card, he used the thumb and index finger of his right hand to yank out a gold Visa card. He walked over to the door that led out of his second floor room. Once there, he opened the door, stepped out onto the walkway overlooking the half empty parking lot and flung the rectangle card through the air.

Back inside the room, Julius then removed the $120.00 from the right front pocket of his pants. He laid the six crisp twenty dollar bills in a straight vertical line on top of the floral bedspread covering one of the double beds in the room. He could hear a woman and man enjoying one another on the other side of the shared wall to his right. The quick squeaking of the bed aroused Julius so much that he began to stroke his dick, trying to time his release with that of the couple a few feet away.

A few minutes later, Julius sprayed his semen onto the dingy green carpet below him.

He then took off his clothes and masturbated again. The sound of the couple was fainter now but he could still hear the low moans of the woman. He came again.

Julius felt the worms' presence digging into him. The images inside his head flickered.

He saw the red-headed man having his way with his mother. He walked around the room trying to stop the images, halt the path of the worms. He saw an image of Grace telling him how sorry she was for the life he endured. There was his mother laughing at him and telling him he was just as fucked up as that beast that raped her. An image of Penelope, the lean sixteen-year-old girl in his third period U.S. History class which Julius fought the urge with sweaty palms five days a week to make advances toward, wearing only white tube socks up to her sharp knees, slid through his head.

The figure of the red-headed man came again. And again. And again. Each time, Julius only could see the back of the man's head. He could see the man's pale white ass moving back and forth, his thin hands holding his mother's butt.

As Julius laid his naked body onto the bed, one of the twenty dollar bills slowly floated to the floor. Julius grabbed at both his forearms, scratching at each.

Get the fuck off of me. Get off. No more.

The worms continued to squirm. Each one becoming bigger, exposing large silver, triangle shaped teeth. Each worm finding its own pocket inside of Julius to begin the feeding. Julius felt the sickening texture of hundreds of worms entering his mouth and slithering down his throat and out of his ass. The scene of Diana Ross in "Lady Sings The Blues" cuffed in a clean, white straight jacket rested behind his eyes.

How did I come from you? Tell me you fuckin' monster. How can it be I'm from you?

Get the fuck off me, now … now get off me. Get the fuck off me. What do I do—where do I go?

How? What … get the fuck get off off off me it hurts, you're hurting me … get off give me relief yeah yeah yeah that's what I need give it to me. End me. End me here so my shit of a life stops today.

I'm done fighting you … too many of you—don't hurt me please don't hurt me. Go away … who in the hell is that?

No, oh no oh no what in the hell …

he's too big

too big he's going to swallow me

wait wait I won't sleep with prostitutes anymore I promise I won't

you're too fucking big oh shit don't chew on me

don't please I won't all I ever wanted was the truth

look at me

my beautiful Grace gone

my son Joey

eat the other fuckin' redhead eat him not me shit stop

you're chewing me up stop it please

no no no fuck it just kill me

I'm done here

my mother is ashamed of me I don't blame her now

you can trace me back to the redness of crazy

before you devour my flesh tell them all how fucked up I really am

tell them all I lived every day seconds away from insanity

get it right seconds away from going crazy

blurring the lines

you win here your worms been inside me too long thought I could flush you out of me in them massage parlors wrapped in the strong legs of a woman and shooting my semen here and there

thought I could outlive you all

where did you come from because there are too many of you

you won't leave me be will you and so I know now you are

the disgusted glare I stay clear of in my mother's presence

you the uneasiness firing around my pale shell

I know you now

while you eat from the inside I've taken care of the eating on the outside

then I think about courage

pride

the ability to change
but I can't change where I come from
red hair sits atop my head too
red genes move in me too
so eat me up like you plan to
it don't hurt no more

Julius still lay atop the bed in his motel room whispering to himself over and over again *it don't hurt no more*. Then he stood straight up on the bed and looked at himself in the mirror hanging on the wall across from him. Semen stuck to the red hair of his inner thighs. His dick soft and leaning slightly to the left. His stomach growling. The taste of bad breath in his mouth. He met his light brown eyes in the mirror and paused. And then he cried. Not for himself but for Grace and Joey. He cried for his mother. For Jessica.

Julius let his eyes leave the mirror.

It don't hurt no more. It just don't. It don't hurt no more.

He laid himself onto the stiff, green carpet in his motel room and curled his body into a fetal position.

- KATRINA -

Mommy, let me take you home.

Katrina refused the ride offered to her by her daughter. She was too embarrassed to let Veronica and especially her granddaughter see the shabby motel room she called home.

No, no you take Sabrina home.

Vic's Motel was a haven for prostitutes. The rooms of the motel formed a U shape. Throughout the day men in cars drove into the motel's parking lot hoping to find a lady who was on duty. The ladies peeked out from behind heavy, dingy brown curtains and waved their tricks into the room. Some ladies, upon spotting a car entering the parking lot, opened their doors so her potential client could get a look at her. Many of the women selling their bodies were addicted to meth.

Before Katrina opened the door to her room, she glanced back behind her.

She thought she saw the North Star twinkle at her in the dark blue sky. She took a deep breath in and released it back into the air. Then she unlocked the door and entered her room.

The first thing Katrina did was turn on the TV. She jabbed at the remote control until she found a channel displaying a white man, dressed in an elegant burgundy gown with a large gold crucifix hung around his chest, yelling that *only God has the abundance to deliver his children into the light.*

She then sat down on the double bed in front of the television and undressed herself leaving only a black scrunchy in her hair. She plopped two fluffy white pillows up against the headboard and sat back. She raised the volume on the television and then tossed the remote control onto the floor. Sitting on the nightstand to her right was an unopened bottle of vodka, a nearly empty bottle of tequila, and four warm beers.

First to go were the beers.

The man kept yelling. Katrina felt as if he was sitting next to her on the bed. Next went the Vodka, She drank it straight from the bottle. She liked the burn it made in her as the liquid slid down and into her bloodstream.

The white man kept on talking.

God has a way people of knowing your ugliness. All the ugliness you run from. God knows. Yes sir. God knows. Now I can testify that I know a good God. I know a God that has the power to redeem even the most lost souls amongst us. Katrina continued to drink while the white man continued to talk.

Ask yourself, can God help you in your time of need? Well, can he? You may not believe so but God knows how to deliver you into thy kingdom come.

When the vodka was gone so was Katrina.

The motel maid found Katrina on Monday morning sprawled across the bed. The maid immediately walked the short distance to the office to get Vic. Vic entered the room and cringed at the smell of vomit. He could see that there was still a great deal of vomit sitting in Katrina's open mouth.

Vic turned to speak to the maid who was not the slightest bit unnerved. She had made two similar discoveries like this one before at Vic's Motel.

I'll make some calls. Don't worry right now of even trying to clean up this shit. Bitch probably just had too many demons up on her.

- J U L I U S -

Julius had no idea what time it was. He still lay curled up, his arms hugging himself, on the carpet. Naked. Cold. He had to take a shit but didn't feel like it. Lying on the carpet was all he could manage.

Today is Monday.

He knew he would have to make a call to his school to inform the office to contact a substitute teacher; he wouldn't be in today.

What time is it? Get up Julius get up don't want to I'll just stay here lost in step ain't going to work ain't can't get up regroup ... The image of his father wouldn't leave him. The red hair. The violent glare of hate this man must have given his mother. Even in his state of mind, Julius reasoned that his pursuit of escape from life, his fantasy, his yearning to be touched by women selling their time and bodies was his destiny. All the lust, depression, and masturbation were just numbing him out until bringing him to the identity of his father.

I come from that fucked up thing of a man rapist sadistic muthafucka get your ass up Julius ...

He raised his head to look about the room.

Where am I?

The worms were not there. He looked at the clock.

5:17 AM.

Ache and sorrow kept him on the carpet. He made no attempt to rise.

I'm just going to sleep all I got in me sorry Joey your dad is fucked up you have a good mother though real good mother I can't be with you in a consistent way my staying power all messed up don't think I'm crazy Joey depressed scared weak that's part of me don't think I'm crazy Joey I'm not crazy man … he is crazy.

Julius closed his eyes. Julius opened his eyes. Julius closed his eyes.

His students were standing outside the door. There were more than thirty teenage girls and boys. Backpacks flung over some of their shoulders. Boys in baggy cords and jeans.

Girls huddled up. Julius could hear their conversation.

Is Mr. Holiday coming today or what?

He's late again.

Whatever.

It's cold out here too.

Julius opened his eyes.

7:28 AM.

He stood up and walked the short distance to the small round table that sat in front of the room's window. His keys, some change, and his cell phone were there. He picked up the cell phone, flipped it open and called work.

215

Dunbear High School, this is Judie.

Hi Judie it's Julius.

Hi Julius.

Judie I'm not going to be able to make it in today. Sorry for the late notice, I just don't feel good.

Did you call the subline?

No ... I ... no, I ...

We'll take care of it down here. Any directions you want to leave for the sub or your students?

Just have my first three periods keep reading and discussing chapter 9 in the textbook.

And what about your other two periods?

I don't know. Tell the sub to get a video from the library. I'm sorry ... I ...

I'll let the sub know. Hope to see you tomorrow. Anything else Julius?

That's it.

Take care of yourself. Bye now.

Bye Judie.

What now Julius what now?

He could feel a surge bulging in his stomach and making its way up to his neck. He felt Jessica's muffled screams in his head. He grimaced in shame for allowing himself to lie on the top bunk as Uncle Bobbie made his sister his little lady. Jessica never told anyone. Uncle Bobbie would slide his weight into Julius three times too. Julius was nine. He remembered being home alone with his uncle. He remembered being locked in the bathroom seeing his reflection looking back at him; seeing Uncle Bobbie hunched behind him, half of his penis penetrating his anus.

Julius walked into the tiny bathroom, took a shit, dressed, and headed to the Cascade Bridge. The images swirling around in his head were too much to hold. Uncle Bobbie's face and the wild, red-haired man scaring the shit out of his mother sitting in him like sharp blades. Julius didn't know which one to turn on himself first.

The Fiesta cruised along. The sun was up. Julius drove with the morning commuters. Stop and go. Every so often Julius looked to his left and to his right. A woman in a green sedan applying makeup.

A man and a woman in a black pickup. The man reading the newspaper. The woman bobbing her head to music. A man on a cell phone. A man in a suit and tie yawning into the day. Julius was numb.

The slow of the traffic only served to speed up the anxiety overtaking him.

The old Cascade Bridge was one way into Bluechester. City folk called it the picturesque portal into the city. The bridge spanned its large body over the murky water of the Buck River. Constructed during the decade of 1920, it was gothic in appearance. Tons and tons of concrete, painted blue, and cables shooting into the sky gave the historical landmark a surreal beauty.

After more than forty minutes slugging his way with

the morning traffic crunch, Julius veered slightly to the right following the green and white sign that read Cascade Bridge. Most of the cars kept straight taking the expressway into Bluechester. The Fiesta picked up speed. Julius wondered if he had enough gas to make it to the bridge. He opened the flap of his cell phone. Hit the power button. No missed calls. No messages. One vertical battery bar out of three showing in the right corner on the phone.

Julius remembered reading an article in the newspaper about the number of people who jumped off the Cascade. The majority of the suicide jumpers were successful. The article highlighted one jumper who survived the jump which was more than two hundred feet down into the Buck. The man broke both of his legs, his back, suffered a severe concussion, and crushed every rib in his body. But he survived. He was quoted in the paper as saying he realized right when he jumped that he didn't really want to die and now given a second chance he would take full advantage of his second life. Julius thought the man was full of shit.

Julius caught the blueness of the bridge dancing and glistening with the sun's beams as he approached.

Beautiful.

He parked the Fiesta in a parking lot used by visitors who wanted to walk the narrow, paved path across the nearly one-mile long Cascade. He grabbed his cell phone.

Opened the glove box. Took out a picture of Joey opening Christmas presents a year ago. Joey's smile and bright eyes made him look away from the photo. He stuffed the 4 x 6 picture into his front pocket and walked. He looked over his shoulder and felt a presence behind him, pushing him on. He looked down at the pavement. Thought he saw worms. Thought he saw a large cobra wink at him. Then a hiss. Two pointed teeth on him. Then he saw hundreds of cobras lined up behind the large cobra. All of them moving in for the eating. His mind raced.

Grace. Goodbye. Jess. Peace. Sorry Momma. Fuck you Bobbie.

A Tracy Chapman song made its way into his limbs.

I got a fast car …

Lyle… You got it together.

Joey. Live better than me.

To jump from the Cascade was an easy task. Only a four-foot brick wall separated a walker from the cold water below. Julius, walking quickly, was approaching the bridge's center. Every ten feet or so he glanced over his right shoulder. The cobras still moving in on him. The big one in front grew larger. It grew hands that reached for Julius. Julius frowned at the blue sky. His sweaty palms hung at his sides. Then his mind quieted. The warmth of the morning sun grabbed at him. The humming sounds coming from cars and trucks driving across the Cascade hovered and circulated in the air. Time slowed. And then the voices in his head spoke.

Jump muthafucka jump! Uncle Bobbie left him.

I am done with you Julius. I love you but I am done with you. Grace left him.

I don't blame you Julius. Jessica's voice sat on his chest.

Julius, it's hard to love you. You hear me? His mother's glare rested on his heart.

He put his cell phone down on the white pavement.

Through his eyes he was surrounded by cobras. They were everywhere. Biting his flesh. Hissing. Biting. Biting. He tasted his own warm blood. The big cobra attempted to swallow him whole. Julius stopped fighting. The tearing of his flesh made him close his eyes. Hundreds of cobras eating out their own section of his departed body.

This is what death looks like.

He pulled the wrinkled picture of Joey from his pants. Kissed the image of his son and set it under the cell phone. And then Julius was a silhouette.

Falling.

Falling.

Falling.

Towards the Buck River.

Falling.

Falling.

Falling.

He raised his hands over his head, spread his legs, and screamed.

-VERONICA-

Veronica vigorously stroked the hard dick of a man in a wheelchair. She wished he would hurry up and cum so she could get home to have dinner with Sabrina. The man kept saying go faster. Go faster. Come on faster. Use two hands. Veronica picked up the pace. As the man enjoyed his moment, Veronica daydreamed of her mother.

She and Uncle Roman met at the hospital to claim Katrina's body. Her mother's death was a relief. At least that was what she told herself. But as time passed, it had been more than six months now, Veronica began to assess her life. She enrolled in a community college. She became more selective in the clients she offered her services to. Her plan was to leave the escort business within a year.

The man saying—I'm about to cum—broke her daydream.

Can I squirt it on your breasts?

Can't do that.

I'll give you a big tip. I'm real close.

Veronica removed her purple bra and pushed her breasts close to the man's penis.

When he finished, Veronica immediately walked away from the man. Once at the bathroom sink, she wet one of the white towels that hung on the silver towel rack. She caught herself in the mirror.

This shit is going to kill me.

She heard the man's voice.

Can we do it again? I'll pay you for it.

Veronica examined her face in the mirror. She saw her mother mixed in the reflection with her.

Her mother's voice whistled in her ears. *You better learn to deal little girl.* She walked back over to the man.

I have to be somewhere in thirty minutes.

That's all I need.

The man reached for Veronica's ass.

No sir, no you don't.

What?

I need to see some money first.

- GRACE -

The UPS driver sat a box on the front porch of Grace's home and rang the door bell before heading back to his truck. Grace put down the book she was reading and got up from the couch to get the door.

Thank you.

The driver smiled and drove away. Grace first saw the turquoise return label on the left of the box. Bostonville Press the first line read. Joey walked out of the office adjacent to where Grace was.

UPS mom?

My book is here, Joey. Can you please get me the scissors from the office?

Got 'em right here.

Grace love-smiled her son.

Here.

Thank you, Joey.

Open it mom.

Okay. Okay.

Grace neatly cut the clear tape away from the box until she could pull both flaps up to reveal her book. On the cover of the book was a drawing of a man climbing up a ladder. The ladder was submerged in deep water.

The right hand of the man, elongated in exaggeration, reached towards a brick wall just out of his grasp. The words:

Trying

To

Get

Over

ran down the right side of the thin book followed by

A collection of prose and poetry

by Grace Holiday

Grace handed Joey one of the books.

This is for you son.

It had been more than a year since Julius escaped into the Buck River. And Grace cried when she opened the book to its dedication page.

for Julius, may you find your healing in the falling.

Grace

This book is for Dad, right mom?

Yes son, this one here is for your dad.

GHOST MAN

- A C K N O W L E D G M E N T S -

Writers never create a book in isolation. While it does take the writer to sit with the narrative and create the vision, the completion of a novel does not take place without the support from others. It is this community that inspires, and I need to thank those for helping this book find its place in the world:

Charles Rice-González, Natalia Menendez, Jonathan Brennan, and Wendy Mazuelos Langford for reading early drafts of the book and for providing rich and loving feedback. And too: Colleen Mills, Louise Hammonds, Douglas Martin, Bushra Rehman, Wendy Chin-Tanner, Chris Millis, Shawn Syms, Bhanu Kapil, Bryan Borland (who believes in this vision), Chris Abani, Larry Compagnoni, Megan Guidry, Annmarie Lockhart, Bruce Guernsey, Matthew Quick, Lee Herrick, Seth Pennington, Sarah Rawlinson, and El Monie.

Those before me and still writing today guide my craft and I must thank the following people:

James Baldwin and Richard Wright, who both broke me open to all possibilities.

Zora Neale Hurston, whose prose is pure and moves beyond the mask, to guide.

Michael Ondaatje, grace on the page. A true force.

Theresa Tran, Rebecca Tran, Guillermo Mazuelos, Carmen Mazuelos, Edward Gills, Ron Levy, Adriana Tavernise, Synnika Lofton, Robert Dewar, Wil Cason, Robert Quintero, and Jennifer Nannie.

And thank you to Leslie Moore for somewhere beautiful.

-THE AUTHOR-

Donnelle McGee is the author of *Shine*, a novella, and *Naked*, a collection of poetry. He earned his MFA from Goddard College. He is a faculty member at Mission College in Santa Clara, California. His work has appeared in *Controlled Burn*, *Colere*, *Haight Ashbury Literary Journal*, *Home Planet News*, *Iodine Poetry Journal*, *Permafrost*, *River Oak Review*, *The Spoon River Poetry Review*, and *Willard & Maple*, among others. His work has also been nominated for a Pushcart Prize. Donnelle lives in Sacramento and Turlock, California.

-THE PRESS-

Sibling Rivalry Press is an independent press based in Little Rock, Arkansas. Its mission is to publish work that disturbs and enraptures. This book was published in part due to the support of the Sibling Rivalry Press Foundation, a non-profit private foundation dedicated to assisting small presses and small press authors.

CPSIA information can be obtained at www.ICGtesting.com
Printed in the USA
BVOW06s1231301115

428863BV00008B/90/P